STRANDED WITH PRINCE CHARMING

EVER AFTER
BOOK 3

LAUREN SMITH

Copyright © 2022 by Lauren Smith

Cover Art by Angela Haddon

Cover Photography by Sara Eire

ISBN: 978-1-958196-68-7 (e-book edition)

ISBN: 978-1-958196-69-4 (print edition)

live like
there is no
Midnight

ONCE UPON A TIME…

THERE WAS A PRINCESS CURSED WITH A
FROZEN HEART, BUT TRUE LOVE'S KISS
COULD SAVE HER IF ONLY SHE WAS BRAVE
ENOUGH TO LOVE…

Gstaad, Switzerland

Gstaad, Switzerland
Roarke Covington was trapped at the North Pole. All that was missing were little elves and reindeer wandering around. Okay, so maybe it wasn't actually the North Pole, but it felt like it, with snow everywhere and the Christmas-like feel to the shops and hotels on every street. He wasn't a fan of Christmas. He always spent it alone and, if he was honest, miserable.

Roarke took in the sight of the Swiss town of Gstaad from where he stood on the street outside his hotel. It was an ideal vacation place with soft, powdery ski slopes, fancy restaurants, and fairytale–like hotels tucked into the base of the idyllic Alps. Unlike other similar destinations, Gstaad retained an air of exclusivity which drew in celebrities and rich travelers from all over the world.

A woman in a skintight ski suit, was chatting loudly on her phone with long, fake nails, overly puffy lips and nearly white blond hair extensions as she walked past him. The slight frown on his lips became more prominent. Roarke was old-world, old-school and old-class money from the East Coast even though he now lived in Chicago. He despised the pop princess icons with bleached hair and fake breasts, and the steroid-fueled boy toys that came with them. He hated the Hollywood actors who came here with their mistresses and the rich families that had made money from questionable means... In other words, he hated the world he'd been born into. He would never come to a place like this by choice. No matter how beautiful it was, it was full of people he didn't want to socialize with.

"Fucking Thad." He cursed the name under his breath. He had lost in a game of poker to an old prep school classmate named Thad Worthington last month and agreed to go to Switzerland over Christmas to help him on a real estate deal. He always honored the terms of a bet when he lost, but that didn't mean he liked doing it.

He slung his leather weekender bag over one

shoulder and walked up the entrance to the Hotel Gstaadorhoff. It wasn't the most expensive place he could have stayed, but it was where all the clients who were meeting to discuss the deal planned to stay. The streets were crowded with tourists and skiers. Christmas festivities were already underway. Roarke *hated* Christmas.

The wooden lodge-like frame of the hotel's entrance loomed over him as he dodged a trio of snow bunnies. The girls giggled at him and wiggled their hips in expensive ski suits as they hobbled past him in the snow. Most men would have jumped at the chance to follow those girls and offer to buy them a drink in hopes of it leading somewhere private. Not him. Roarke would bet his life that not one of them actually knew how to ski. He wanted to be with an authentic woman; if she didn't know how to ski, that was fine. But people who posed as something other than what they were didn't interest him.

He entered the lobby and groaned at the site of a wedding party filling the room. That was the last thing he wanted to be around. There was nothing more annoying than a wedding. Such fanfare for so little return on investment. Roarke was not much of a romantic. In fact, only one person ever drew that side out in him, and she was out of his reach. For everyone and everything else, he was anything but romantic. Instead, he was practical, calm, intense. That was who he was. He dodged the wedding party and approached the front desk.

"Welcome to the Hotel Gstaadorhoff." The receptionist smiled at him warmly.

"I have a reservation under Covington." He had been told he would likely have to share a room with the junior lawyer he was supposed to be helping on the real estate deal. It was another thing to add to the long list of his irritations over this entire endeavor.

"Ahh, yes, here we are." The woman made him a set of room keys and he slid his credit card across the counter, which she put into the system. "Your other guest is already checked in."

"Have any of the other guests under these names checked in yet? We're here for a business meeting, and we'll be using a conference room this week with them." He handed the receptionist a sheet with the names of the other parties on it.

"Give me one moment." She checked for the names, then shook her head. "No, none of these people have checked in yet, sir."

"Thank you. Could you call my room when they arrive?"

"Of course, sir."

He'd already started to turn away when the receptionist spoke up again. "The weather will be quite severe here over the next few nights; please be careful outside. They will be clearing the ski slopes tonight in order to maintain safety. It should be better during the day. I'm not sure if the airports will be closed, in case you're waiting on your guests to fly in."

"Right," Roarke muttered as he glanced out the windows at the picturesque mountains. He actually liked Gstaad's scenery. He didn't get to spend much time at places like this. Being able to look at the Alps was one of the few benefits of losing the bet to Thad. He followed the signs to the elevator and headed up to his room.

He pulled out his cell and texted Thad, letting him know he'd landed and would be meeting up with the junior lawyer soon. Normally, he was on the opposite side of the table from Thad on business deals because he worked at a law firm that usually represented the other side in any real estate transactions that Thad participated in. A real estate tycoon, Thad ran a successful company with his father. They exclusively used the lawyers from Pimms & Associates to represent their company because Thad's best friend Jared was the senior real estate attorney at Pimms. Normally, Jared would have handled a deal like this, but he was busy spending Christmas with his wife and new baby girl, so a junior lawyer from Pimms was handling it. Thad apparently didn't trust this rookie lawyer, so he'd called in the favor Roarke owed him.

All Roarke had to do was show up here, help this associate attorney out and show the kid the ropes, as well as make sure Thad got a good deal on the property he wanted to buy. And then Roarke and Thad would be square.

I'll never drink and play poker with that bastard again.

They weren't friends, but they'd recently run into each other in Vegas at a private card game and when Thad had challenged him to play, he couldn't resist. So he'd sat down and played, and he'd *lost*. Rather than take the chips he was owed, Thad had demanded a favor to be called in when he needed it.

Roarke pressed the key card to the door. When the green light flashed, he turned the handle and stepped inside. The room was bright and clean with light walnut wood paneling on the walls and a pair of twin beds along the wall, only four feet apart. The bathroom door was closed, and he heard the sound of running water.

The other lawyer had to be in the shower. The guy probably had jet lag like he did. Roarke traveled internationally a lot, but he didn't sleep on planes that well, even in first class. He always felt like shit the first day.

He dropped his bag on the floor and then lay back on one of the beds.

He chose the one that was near the window, which led to a small balcony that overlooked the snowy mountainside. It would be nice to wake up in the morning and have a good view of the scenery. The snowy landscape was somehow calming. He folded his hands behind his head, crossed his legs at the ankles and shut his eyes. If the rookie lawyer had a problem with him getting the primo bed, too bad.

He wasn't sure how long he'd dozed off for before a screech jerked him awake. Bolting upright, he found a nearly naked woman standing in the bathroom's doorway. All that covered her was a flimsy hotel towel.

"Roarke?" The woman gasped his name as both of her hands clutched at the edge of the towel, holding it tightly together at her breasts and thighs. It took him another moment to pull his eyes off the most gorgeous pair of legs he'd ever seen before he could look at the woman's face.

Wet blonde hair hung in long burnished gold strands down her shoulders, and soft, startled blue eyes stared back at him.

Holy shit...

"Shana? What the hell are you doing here?" he demanded as he got to his feet.

"Me? What about *you*? This is *my* room." Those

lovely eyes were lit with fury. God, he had always thought Shana Pimms was the most beautiful woman he'd ever seen, but she'd been off limits for years. She was the daughter of his biggest legal competitor, and she was also Jared's ex-girlfriend, which meant she was completely untouchable. Still, it didn't stop a man from wanting her with a barely controlled madness.

"Roarke, seriously, what the hell are you doing in my room?" she asked more quietly this time, and he realized how he must have scared her by being there.

Wait a damn minute—this was *his* room.

"When I checked in at the front desk, they gave me a key to this room and said it was mine."

"Okay, we'll figure *that* out in the minute. I meant, what are you doing here in Switzerland?" she asked, still clutching her towel. He was a bastard for wishing desperately that her grip would slip so he'd get to see what he'd fantasized about for years.

"I lost a bet," he said.

"A bet? What does that mean?" She arched a dark gold brow at him. God, the expression was adorable and sexy but also intimidating. It was an intoxicating combination.

"I lost a bet in a game of poker to Thad, and my repayment was to help some associate lawyer of Jared's in negotiating the hotel purchase. But it was supposed to be a man I was meeting."

"You were supposed to meet Braden Wallace?"

"Er... Yeah, that was the name Thad texted me."

Shana closed her eyes and let out a long-suffering sigh. "Great, just great. My dad sent me here to cover for Braden. He had a family emergency. I didn't know Thad was sending someone to help him."

"So we'll just call the hotel front desk, and I'll get another room." The last thing he wanted was to stay in another room, but sleeping so close to Shana was a temptation he'd be hard pressed to resist acting on. He needed to do the right thing and just get another room, even though every fantasy he'd had for years involved sharing a room and a *bed* with this woman. Though his back was turned toward her, he could still feel her presence as she moved near the bathroom.

He picked up the phone on the small nightstand between the two beds and dialed zero.

"This is the front desk. How may I help you?"

"Hi, this is Mr. Covington from room 208. There seems to be a bit of a mix-up. I need a new room; I can't share one with Miss Pimms."

"Oh ... I understand, but Mr. Covington, we are completely booked up. We don't have a spare room we can move you into."

Roarke's heart gave an excited little jump at the thought that now he had no choice but to stay with her. But the receptionist shattered that hope quickly.

"I could call a few other hotels in the city for you."

"Yes, please do that, thank you." He hung up and met Shana's questioning gaze. She was standing a little closer and the smell of her soap, clean and vanilla scented, drifted across the room. It made him a little dizzy with desire, but he had to stay focused. He'd never been more aware of anyone in this life than he was of her right now.

"What did they say?"

"This hotel is booked. They're checking other places in town for me."

"What a mess," Shana muttered. Then she seemed to remember she was practically naked. "Do you mind if I grab a few things from my bag and—"

"Not at all." He sat back on the bed again and lay back once more, closing his eyes. He listened to the rustling about the room and, because he was an asshole, he peeked one eye open to see her retrieving a gossamer thin set of bra and panties from her suitcase.

Fuck... That was his punishment for peeking. He would give anything to know what she looked like in that pale pink lacy set of lingerie. She closed the bathroom door to change inside, while he retrieved his phone from his pocket and sent Thad a text.

Roarke: Tell me you didn't know.

A moment later, Thad responded.

Thad: Know what?

Roarke: *That I'd be rooming with Shana, not Braden Wallace at this hotel in Switzerland.*

He almost laughed when a call came a second later. He got up and stepped out onto the balcony, closing the glass doors behind him before he answered. It was damned cold outside, but he didn't want Shana to hear.

"What do you mean you're rooming with Shana?" Thad demanded. He never had dated her, but he protected her like a sister.

"I mean, unless another hotel has a spare room, I'm bunking with the beautiful bombshell ex-girlfriend of your best friend. I'm not complaining, by the way."

"You're such a dick, you know that right?" Thad growled.

"I know," Roarke chuckled. "But it's not my fault. Jared sent her to replace Braden, who had a family emergency."

"Shit, I didn't know. I've been busy with Veronica. We're planning a Christmas at Disney. I'm going to propose to her, and it needs to be perfect. Jared's busy with Felicity and Hayley."

"Yeah, yeah, you're both going to be old married men now with kids," Roarke snorted.

He was the same age as Jared and Thad, but for the first time he felt weirdly behind somehow because he didn't have a wife and 2.5 kids plus a minivan. Not that he would be caught dead in a minivan. He'd get some badass SUV to drive the kids around in. Wait... Since when did he think about kids? God, Jared and Thad were rubbing off on him in the worst way.

"So how is it that you're rooming with her? Why don't you get your own room?" Thad asked, as if Roarke hadn't been smart enough to try that.

"We tried that. No rooms are left at this inn," he joked. "We might be sleeping in the stables..." He couldn't keep from grinning and was glad Thad couldn't see his face.

Thad made an angry huffing sound that filled Roarke with boyish glee.

"Then stay somewhere else in town."

"I'm trying to, but it might not happen," Roarke warned with a smug chuckle.

"Then sleep in the fucking lobby, Covington. Shana is off limits."

Roarke pictured Shana with her dewy skin fresh from the shower and wearing nothing but that little hotel towel... That image would occupy his dreams for the next decade.

"Actually, I'd say nothing is off limits." He leaned on his forearms on the balcony railing and watched the people below eating at the outdoor restaurant on the first floor.

"If you do anything to her, I will end you, Covington."

Roarke frowned. "Why do you and Jared treat her like she's made of glass? She's not some fragile princess to protect."

Thad was quiet a long moment. Only his breathing on the other end of the line assured Roarke he was still on the phone.

"I shouldn't even be saying anything to you, but Shana's father is a controlling asshole. Ever since she and Jared failed to do the whole 'marry and run the firm as husband and wife' thing, Shana has had a difficult relationship with her dad. He's a cold, unfeeling asshole. We're just trying to watch out for her."

Roarke knew exactly how it felt to have a man controlling your life and all of your decisions, and none of it was what was best for you. He'd had to break away from his father's control, and it hadn't been easy. Knowing Shana faced the same situation left a heaviness in his belly.

"I come from a long line of asshole fathers, Worthington. If anyone understands what bullshit a person puts up with under those circumstances, it's me. I wouldn't do anything to hurt her."

"You may have a point," Thad reluctantly admitted. "But I'm serious. Do not pull some one-night stand crap and leave her with a broken heart. She is a class act and deserves better than you."

"She does," Roarke agreed. Shana was classy.

She was beautiful, but that beauty paled in comparison to her compassion and intelligence. It always puzzled him that she'd ended up in real estate law. She had a large heart, one suited for the tougher areas of family law, instead of property transactions. Any lawyer could learn to do real estate. But to have an instinct above and beyond to work with *people*—that was a rare gift. He'd had the pleasure of seeing her in action in court more than once, and each time he found himself turned on by her brain, not just her body.

"So we have a deal?" Thad asked.

"I'll behave, but if she decides she wants me, then she'll have me. The lady deserves to get what she wants." Roarke hung up, picturing Thad growling before he likely threw his phone across the room. Roarke pocketed his cellphone, stepped back into the room and resumed his place on the bed farthest from the bathroom. When the door opened, he bit his lip to hide a smile.

What the hell was Roarke Covington doing here? Shana stared at the closed bathroom door a long second before she let the towel drop to the floor so she could put her clothes on. She knew logically that he had explained why he was here—because of some bet he had lost and agreed to help Braden. But still...

Roarke was the last person she expected to see. He wasn't known for being *that guy,* the dependable friend. Hell, he wasn't even Thad or Jared's friend. He had gone to school with Thad, Jared and their friend Angelo at some fancy East Coast prep school, but he had never been a part of their crowd. He and Jared both ended up at Creighton Law, where Shana had met Jared and fallen hard for him. But Roarke had always been there, lurking in the background like some dark prince in a twisted fairytale. He was a bad boy. Every girl knew the type. The one who could melt your panties with a smile one minute and break your heart in the next.

That was the very last kind of guy she needed to be around, because bad boys were her weakness. Jared had been too sweet; it was one of the reasons they had never worked as a couple. They got together, broke up and got together again, but there was always something missing. It had pissed off her father that she had broken up with Jared that final time and had stayed broken up. Now Jared was married to a great girl, Felicity, a museum curator, and they had the most adorable baby in the world. Maybe other people thought it was weird, but Shana and Jared were still good friends, and now she and Felicity were friends, Shana had somehow become Aunt Shana to their little baby, Hayley.

Life was good. *Mostly.*

Her father was still pressuring her to step up and take over his real estate book of clients. She didn't want that life, but she didn't see much of a way out unless she left her father's firm. Doing that would be like divorcing herself from her family, even though it wasn't much of a family.

She was lonely. She'd never been comfortable with casual sex, at least not on a regular basis, so she was alone more often than not. Okay, she was alone *a lot.* Sometimes she truly enjoyed being free of the worries and responsibilities that came with a relationship. She learned a lot about herself, about who she was and what she wanted in her life now. She also wanted to share it with someone.

But finding someone who liked her for who she was, not for her paycheck, or who her family was, wasn't easy. Her long work hours and her own lack of self-confidence didn't help her romantic chances. She wished she could just let go of her worries, fling open the bathroom door, shove Roarke onto the bed, climb up his body and lose herself in him and the pleasure of sleeping with him.

He offered the delicious bad boy temptation that few women could resist. A woman knew a man like him would be so good in bed. But it was what might happen afterward that worried her. She couldn't just bang him and then go on about her day, no matter how much she wished she could.

Her cellphone, which lay on the bathroom counter, vibrated. She quickly answered and heard Jared's voice.

"You okay? I heard you're currently sharing a room with Prick McGee."

She snorted a little laugh. Prick McGee was Jared's nickname for Roarke.

"I'm fine. He's been nice. He was as shocked as I was."

"Well, don't worry, we'll get you a separate room immediately. Just keep your distance from him."

For some reason, Shana resented Jared's fatherly tone. They'd almost been engaged once, and now he was treating her like a misbehaving child.

"I'll be fine," she repeated.

"Good. You don't need to spend time around guys like Roarke. They have only one goal, and you're too good for a guy like that."

Too good. Yeah, that was the problem. He treated her like she was perfect, like she wanted to be perfect. Shana wanted to be bad. She wanted to misbehave and sleep with the sexy bad boys. She didn't want to be so... restrained.

"I've got to go. I'll call you later. Tell Felicity and Hayley I said hi." Then she hung up on Jared.

A moment later her cellphone screen flashed with a text from Jared's wife.

Felicity: Heard you are rooming with Roarke. He's soooo hot. Don't waste a night with that body of his. 😉 ***P.S. I want details later!***

The emoji of a winky face made Shana smile. This was why she and Felicity were friends. Felicity understood her more than anyone else in her life right now. Felicity was smart, funny, and hardworking, all the things that Shana valued in a friend. It didn't matter about her past with Jared; Felicity wasn't jealous or worried. She knew that she and her daughter were Jared's whole world. That fact gave Felicity the confidence to see Shana as a friend, not competition.

Shana let out a sigh as she knew she couldn't put off facing Roarke any longer. She opened the door and found him lounging on the bed farthest from her and the bathroom, idly flipping through the channels on the TV. He wore dark slacks and a pale cream sweater that hugged his broad shoulders and hung a little looser around his trim waist. The man was *gorgeous*. She'd never been able to deny that. He had dark brown hair that had russet undercurrents in the sunlight, and his eyes were warm brown that were quick to heat with mischief. He was her deep, dark fantasy, one she'd been too afraid to think about.

He shut off the TV when he noticed her.

"Bad news... There are no other rooms available in the whole town."

"You're kidding."

His sensual lips curved into a devil-may-care grin.

"I wish I was. They said something about a Christmas festival meaning all the other places, even the lowliest of motel kind of places are completely booked up for the next few days," Roarke said.

"So what you're saying is..."

"You've got a roommate." He winked at her. "And I promise I don't snore."

"What?" She stared at him blankly. "You can't be serious—"

"Afraid so, honey. You're stuck with me."

He stood up and came toward her, and she was all too aware of how tall he was. She wasn't short at five foot seven, but next to Roarke she felt delicate and feminine.

"Roomie?" He held out his hand.

She reluctantly took it. A flash of heat sizzled between their hands.

"Roomie," she echoed. She had a sense that the next few days were going to test her willpower in ways she'd never been tested before.

"Care to grab a meal while we wait for the others to arrive?"

"Sure." She could use the distraction. The less time she spent near Roarke and a bed would be good. But the smug grin on his face made her suspect he was thinking the same thing. That made her skin flush with heat.

Oh, yeah ... This is going to be a huge problem.

2

The look on Shana's face when he had told her she had a roommate was priceless. He wasn't lying though. The hotel front desk had called him seconds before she'd emerged from the bathroom. Apparently between the looming bad weather and the Christmas festivities, the little village was completely booked up.

Shana gathered her purse and coat. She wore a pair of black, slim-fitting trousers and a cozy, pale blue sweater with weather boots. She had smartly assumed they would be going out for their meal. She'd dried her hair and pulled it up into a long blonde ponytail, and Roarke had the sudden image of grabbing her ponytail and winding her hair around his fist while he kissed her hard. He wanted to do that, bad. She glanced his way and thankfully couldn't read any of his thoughts, or she would've slapped him.

"Where are we going?" she asked as they exited the room and headed for the elevator.

"I was thinking La Bagatelle. It's in another hotel, the Hôtel Le Grand Chalet. The front desk will be able to call a cab for us."

As they stepped into the elevator, there were quite a few other people inside. Roarke placed his hands on Shana's shoulders and gently drew her back a few steps to make room for other people. It put her body flush against his, and he could smell a soft vanilla scent drift up from her hair. He leaned forward slightly and drew in a deep breath. She smelled fantastic, and the pleasure of her scent went straight to his groin. He had to remind himself there were other people present, which kept him on his best behavior.

He kept his hands on her shoulders the rest of the ride down to the first floor, and as they stepped off he placed a hand on the small of her back, guiding her in front of him. She didn't pull away, and something about that made him smile. Who knew what would happen if he got Shana away from her overprotective white knights? She might actually *like* him. He loved to play the asshole who riled up her friends, but he only did that to get a laugh. With Shana, she'd get the real him, not false bravado, no bullshit, just him.

He helped her into the back of the taxi. The driver navigated the snowy streets carefully before stopping in front of the hotel. It sat at the base of another scenic mountain, even bigger than the one their hotel was nestled beneath. In the darkness of the snow and trees, the golden glowing lights of the chalet were beckoning with their warmth.

"This place is beautiful," Shana murmured. They climbed the steps to be greeted by a doorman who graciously ushered them inside. They checked their coats at a coat check and then looked around for the restaurant.

"In the summer, they have terrace seating that faces the mountain," Roarke said. "I wish we could be here to see that."

"Me too... I imagine it's all green hills," she sighed. "It makes me think of *The Sound of Music* even though I know that was Austria, not Switzerland."

"The hills are alive," Roarke snorted. "Those lyrics gave me nightmares as a kid."

Shana laughed, the sound utterly adorable. "They *did* not," she insisted.

"The hills are alive. *Alive*," he reiterated and ran his fingertips up her spine, teasing her through the thin cashmere sweater she wore. She jerked and squealed, clearly ticklish. She whirled on him, her face flushed red.

"Oh my God, don't do that!" she hissed. But she was still laughing and completely embarrassed.

"What? Touch you or tickle you?" He emphasized the difference by running his fingers up her spine again. This time, she bumped into him the way a woman does when she's flirting.

"Both." She was frowning as she said that, but Roarke had her number now. She *liked* being touched and tickled.

He raised his hands in mock surrender, and she rolled her eyes.

The restaurant in the chalet was cozy and inviting, with warm wood-paneled ceilings and cream-colored walls. A fireplace in the center of the restaurant was lit with real logs which crackled as they burned. A pair of antique swords crossed over one side of the fireplace mantle, while potted plants covered the low wall separating various parts of the dining room. It felt woodsy and rustic despite the fact that almost everyone in the restaurant was dressed as though they were out for night at the Ritz or the Waldorf-Astoria. The waiter led them to a private table by a window so they could look out at the snowy night. Swirls of glittering snowflakes danced playfully and bounced off the glass, which was frosted at the edges.

"Wow, this place is just incredible..." Shana blushed

as the waiter pushed her chair in as she sat down. Roarke took the seat across from her.

"It is, isn't it? Makes me want to get over to Europe more often."

"Or ever," she added. She ducked her head as though embarrassed.

"Wait..." He gaped at her. "Is this your first time in Europe?"

"How pathetic would it be if I admitted that?" she asked in a soft voice. Her face was suddenly reflected a shy mortification. He felt bad for teasing her.

"It's not pathetic at all," he assured in a tone that matched hers. "I just assumed that your family traveled a lot."

She shook her head. "No, my family doesn't. We stay in Chicago, and we work. All the time. At least, my dad and I do." There was a barely concealed sorrow tinged with bitterness in her words.

Roarke frowned, but held his tongue. He wanted to tell her that was bullshit, that she didn't have to work all the time and if she wanted to explore the world, she had a right to.

"I'm only here because no one else could take Braden's spot but me. Everyone else had cases and court appearances they couldn't reschedule. Jared would've come, but he's really put his foot down when it comes to my father and his workplace demands."

"Not like you," Roarke guessed. He'd heard tales from Jared and Thad about how rude and judgmental her father was. She was told all the time she was never smart enough, never good enough, never fast enough, never billed enough. That kind of subtle abuse could cause serious damage.

"No, not like me." Shana did meet his gaze. She looked instead out the window at the dark snowy night. "Wow, we just jumped straight into the heavy stuff, didn't we?" She gave a little shrug of her shoulders as if she was ready to dislodge the weight off them. "I almost wish you just tried to sleep with me. That I can handle." She chuckled but still wouldn't meet his eyes.

Roarke reached across the table and gently turned her chin so she faced him.

"I would *very much* like to sleep with you, Shana, anytime and anyplace. But don't hide from me. I'm not Jared, Thad or Angelo. I'm not ever going to put you on a pedestal or be disappointed when you show any vulnerability." He smiled. "Besides, people have a habit of falling off pedestals."

Her lips twitched into a ghost of a smile. "Are you saying you don't like perfect women?"

Roarke rolled his eyes. "Perfection is overrated and boring. Give me a real woman with flaws any day. I would never want to hold a woman to those impossible standards. I want her to be herself."

At his words, her eyes fixed on him over the top of her menu, and he didn't quite understand the expression in her gaze, but he didn't look away. He meant what he'd said.

After a moment, her eyes softened and the intensity of her assessing him faded as she relaxed and smiled. The expression nearly knocked his heart out of his chest. It lit her entire face up.

"What are your flaws?" she asked him with a hint of teasing in her lovely eyes. His stomach did a funny little flip.

"Arrogance, of course. When you look as good as me—"

She threw her napkin at him and laughed. "Seriously, Roarke."

Chuckling, he tossed the cloth napkin back at her.

"I have a terrible habit of wanting things that are too good for me. Things I don't deserve." As he said this, he met her eyes—and he knew the second she understood what he was telling her. She was the thing he wanted that he didn't deserve.

"I think we should order food before that poor waiter panics." Shana discreetly nodded her head at the young man hovering a short distance away, his eyes anxiously fixed on their table.

"All right, you're no fun." Roarke grumbled as he signaled the waiter over.

"What would you like to order?" the man asked them.

"Can I have the wild shrimp scampi from South Africa sautéed in garlic and parsley butter?" When she noticed Roarke watching her with a bemused expression, she shrugged. "I love shrimp scampi and I rarely get to eat it."

"You won't get any judgment from me, babe. Eat whatever you want. The whole point of eating is to enjoy the experience." He winked at her and she smiled, even though her face reddened a little.

The waiter scribbled down Shana's order. "And for you, sir?"

"I'll have the sweet bread oxtail raviolis with mushrooms."

"And for your main courses?"

Shana scanned the menu again. "Crispy roasted chicken breast with rosemary."

"And I'll have the saddle of lamb," Roarke added. "Shana, would you like any wine?"

"If you're having some..." she began.

Roarke turned to the waiter. "I'd like a Sauvignon Blanc, whatever you recommend."

"I'd like a rosé, whatever you recommend as well."

"Of course." The waiter made another note on his pad, then collected the menus and left them alone.

"So should we talk about the meeting tomorrow?

What will we say and how will we pitch the purchase offer?" Shana seemed determined to focus on business. It was far less personal and no doubt felt safer for her.

Roarke took a sip of his water and then sighed. "Business it is."

For the rest of the meal, they went back and forth on the various points of Thad's deal memo. Roarke was pleased to see Shana had researched the deal as though she'd been preparing for months rather than twenty-four hours. He had known she was incredibly quick, but if he was being honest, she was even quicker than him. He would have to remember that if he ever faced off against her in negotiations. Roarke had always liked smart women, and if they were smarter than him, all the better. Lots of men dated women that they considered less intelligent than themselves or who had less impressive jobs, because it gave the fragile egos of those men a boost. A real man, in his opinion, earned the love and respect of a smart, hard-working woman instead. That said a hell of a lot more about what kind of man someone was.

The food was exquisite, as he hoped it would be, and he was glad to see Shana was enjoying it too. He had the strongest urge to pamper her. Roarke didn't like her Machiavellian father. Now, he was peeling away layers away of emotional abuse the man had heaped on his daughter, and he hated him even more than he originally had. Shana wasn't a complainer, but every now and then when she spoke, little things slipped out that hinted at her unhappiness and her isolation. It was something he was all too familiar with himself. His own father and mother were East Coast blueblood snobs of the worst kind. He had done much to escape the life they had planned for him. But he wasn't happy, he wasn't fulfilled, the way he expected to feel—and it surprised him to feel a bond with Shana over that.

"Dessert?" the waiter inquired hopefully as they had their plates cleared away. He held out to two small dessert menus and they both quickly perused them.

"I'll take the lemon tart with mango sorbet," Shana decided.

"Same for me."

Roarke liked her food choices and enjoyed dinner with her. Normally when he took women out to dinner, they ate very little and chattered the whole time about things that he couldn't bring himself to be interested in. It wasn't the fault of the women he dated; they just hadn't interested him. But something about Shana was different. She'd always been different. She didn't talk a lot, and he actually wished she would talk *more*. It was like diving into a mysterious, deep-running river. The currents that moved inside her mind fascinated him.

"I suppose we should get back to the hotel and see if the others have checked in."

The others. He had completely forgotten they were supposed to meet the other people involved in the real estate deal. He'd blissfully, and surprisingly, forgotten that he'd been working at all. This had started to feel like a nice vacation with an amazing woman. His good mood deflated at the thought that in a few days this would be over, and it would be back to keeping his distance from her.

"Right. I have to call a cab." He went to the front desk of the hotel and asked the manager to hire an SUV for them. When he returned to the restaurant, he found Shana lightly tracing a fingertip along the frosted edge of the windowpanes, her long blonde ponytail swept idly over one shoulder. She looked so young, so vulnerable. Something in his chest quivered dangerously at the sight of her like that.

"Shana, our car's coming." He offered her his hand as he reached the table. She hesitated and then put her hand in his as she stood up. He let go of her once she was on her feet, but he wished he hadn't. Touching her felt electric. If just a caress of their hands felt like that, what would it be like to kiss her? Roarke would give anything to find out.

Shana climbed into the taxi and Roarke followed her. Their elbows and shoulders touched and briefly their knees bumped. It took every part of her willpower to show no reaction to him. But everything about him made her body burn. Before now, she'd always kept a safe distance from him. She had been dating Jared during law school and then off and on after that, and Roarke had always been a presence in the background. She'd never allowed herself to think about him too much or too long. There was something deliciously forbidden about him, but he'd never been so ... close to her before. He was within reach, and none of her protectors back home were here to guilt her into staying away.

Tonight, she'd indulged in a sumptuous dinner of good food and an even better dessert, all because Roarke had inspired her to let go and just enjoy herself. He made it so easy to not worry about anything. It tempted her to stray to the delicious dark side and share a night of passion with him.

Normally she'd worry about whether a guy even wanted her or not, but with Roarke, she had no doubts.

He had said he *wanted* her. That admission tonight above so many other things had pierced the armor that she had painstakingly built around herself years ago. She shivered and he noticed. Without a word, he put an arm around her shoulders and tucked her against his side.

Oh, to be wanted...

Her mother had never wanted a child. Her father had never wanted a daughter. Jared had never really wanted her as a girlfriend. She'd never been wanted her whole life. Yes, she knew she was smart and pretty enough, but that didn't mean anyone actually *wanted* her.

"Whatever deep thoughts you're having, they're making you frown," Roarke mused. His voice was low, sexy and she imagined that was how he sounded just after he had fucked a woman. He would be lazy with male satisfaction, and his voice would sound just like that.

"I'm allowed to frown," she replied. "Do you know how patronizing it is to be told to smile all the time?"

"No need to be defensive," Roarke said in that almost hypnotic voice of his. "I'm not asking you to smile because you're a woman or because it makes you look pretty. In fact, put some glasses and frown and tell me I have a library book past due, and I might die on the spot with lust."

"What?" She lifted her head to stare at him. "Are you telling me you have librarian fantasies?"

Roarke snorted. "I'm telling you I have *Shana* fantasies. Anything you do would turn me on, woman. *Anything*." He reached over and traced the space between her brows. "Even your frown in the way it creases your brow just here." He continued to stroke her skin, and then he moved his fingertips down her nose to her mouth where he traced her lips.

"I could be your *dirty little secret*," he whispered, and she was mesmerized by his eyes and the heat smoldering in them.

"My dirty little secret?" she breathed.

"Yeah, babe. You use me, take me anyway you want, anytime you want. Thad, Jared and Angelo will never know."

The wicked thought nearly set her ablaze. The three men who protected her like older brothers ... they wouldn't have to know she was sleeping with someone they hated.

"You wouldn't tell them just to piss them off?" She arched her brow.

"Whatever happens between us, that's for us alone, no one else." Roarke said. That honesty she'd seen so often tonight shone clearly again his eyes. She believed him when he said it. It felt like a promise, one she could trust.

"Let me think on it," she finally said. Shana expected him to make some flippant remark about wasting his time. When men asked her out, she liked to take her time and think it over. A lot of men had a problem with that. They acted like she should be grateful she got the offer to go out with them. But not Roarke. He simply traced her lips with his fingers once more. His kissable lips curved in a sexy, smile.

"We have all the time in the world to think about it. This offer is permanently open."

"Permanently? What if you start dating someone?" she asked skeptically. It was the lawyer in her to question everything.

He chuckled. "In the highly unlikely scenario that I'm dating someone else, then no. I don't cheat."

"I thought a guy like—" She cut herself off before she said something unkind.

"A guy like me what?" he asked, his eyes narrowing just the slightest.

"Um..." She bit her lip, wishing she hadn't said anything.

"Just tell me. I won't be angry." His tone was still soft, gently seductive with no hint of warning that he would, in fact, be angry.

"It's just that you strike me as a thrill-seeker. People who cheat usually do so because they like the excitement."

"Ahh..." This time his brow furrowed. "You making me your dirty little secret is the only thrill I need. Besides, I'm very creative in bed. That keeps me completely entertained." That, she completely believed too. He looked like the sort of man who knew every creative position, and had skills with his tongue and hands that would leave a woman screaming for more and more pleasure in his bed. The thought made her entire body quiver with such a violent desperation to experience it that she actually had to hold in a little whimper.

"Think on it. You know where to find me."

This time she laughed. "Yeah, apparently four feet from my bed."

When they arrived at the hotel, the front desk had a message for them.

"What is it?" she asked as Roarke read the note.

"Apparently, the lawyers and the seller from the other side of the real estate transaction are caught at the airport in Berlin. They can't make it here due to blizzard conditions. The negotiations will have to be rescheduled."

"You're kidding." She almost groaned. "We came all this way, and now we've got nothing to show for it."

"Think of it this way... Our hotel is paid upfront by your firm we can't go home for another few days due to the weather and it's almost Christmas. Let's just enjoy the freedom." He waggled his eyebrows playfully, but she saw a offer of something more serious in his eyes, and it made her wonder what he really meant.

Enjoy the freedom? Shana had never heard anyone in her life say that to her. Certainly not her father or even Jared, who was also a workaholic. At least he had been, until he met Felicity. Everyone in her life pushed her to constantly work, be productive, be perfect. It was exhausting.

"By the look on your face, I'm assuming you just haven't let loose in a very long time," Roarke observed.

"Try ever," she said as she rubbed her arms and shivered again. They were standing in the lobby where the cold winter wind blew through each time the front doors opened.

"Let's go back upstairs," Roarke said as they headed for the elevators. "I need to shower, so use the bathroom first if you need to."

When they got back to the room, she brushed her teeth and washed her face before she let him take over the bathroom for his shower. Before he closed the door, he winked at her.

"The door's unlocked, if you decide you want to join me."

Shana rolled her eyes and laughed as he finally shut the door. She listened to the water turn on before she reached for her phone. She sent a text to Jared and

Thad about rescheduling the negotiations, but neither responded. She knew they were both probably spending time with their families, having fun, making Christmas cookies, touring Christmas lights in their neighborhoods—all the things she never did because she would have to do them alone.

Shana sat up in the twin bed and stared at the closed bathroom door.

"Don't be stupid..." she muttered to herself. "It's a bad idea."

But all she could hear in her mind was Roarke saying that he wanted to be her dirty little secret. That forbidden flash of heat raced through her all over again. Could she do it? Engage in fun sex with no expectations? Maybe that's what she needed to get her mind off things. Have mind-blowing sex with Roarke. It would be amazing; she knew it would be.

Even now she stood there listening to the sounds in the shower, imagining how slippery his skin would feel beneath the water, how she'd like to wrap her hand around his cock and stroke him and see his face as he came. She wanted to feel his hands, hard and rough as he explored her, hungry to mark her and claim her with his body. She needed it. Needed it more than she'd ever needed anything in her life.

Please don't let this be a mistake.

She got off her bed and walked toward the bathroom. Her hand rested on the handle a long second before she turned it and opened the door. Warm steam enveloped her as she stepped inside. Through the fogged glass, she saw the outline of Roarke's tall, naked body.

As if sensing her presence, he turned and wiped one hand across the steam on the shower door, and she glimpsed him peering at her. He grinned.

"About damn time." He opened the shower door, and her eyes darkened at the sight of his completely ripped, utterly naked body. Her stomach did a somersault and she sucked in a breath. She knew he'd have a gorgeous body, but this... Roarke Covington had the body of a sex god.

As if reading her thoughts, his kissable lips curved into a devastating smile. "I'm all yours, babe."

Oh yes, he was...

3

Shana slipped out of her boots and socks, then she unbuttoned her jeans and peeled them down her body. Every second she moved, she was aware of Roarke watching her. His gaze on her body felt like a tangible caress. It took a lot of her focus to remove her clothes while the distraction of his gorgeous, dripping body was so close. Rivulets of hot water ran down his body in the way she wanted her hands to do. Everything about him looked hard, and yet she imagined his skin would feel as smooth as silk. Her legs trembled at the thought of how, in just moments, all of that raw power in his body would be directed at pleasuring her.

She stepped out of her jeans and then lifted off her sweater. She wore only a sheer pair of panties and a demi-cup bra. She didn't usually wear such sexy under-wear, but she'd packed it on a whim and tonight she had wanted to feel sexy at dinner. And that had a lot to do with Roarke. She crossed her arms over her chest a little, feeling suddenly, terribly shy. She wasn't usually one to striptease. Roarke moved to the open shower door, his look full of scorching heat as he waited for her to join him.

"You're fucking beautiful," he whispered the words reverently. It was his tone, the honesty of his response, that emboldened her to shimmy out of her panties and unclasp her bra and drop it onto the floor.

Roarke held out a hand to her, like a dark Hades beckoning Persephone into his lair in the netherworld. Like any self-respecting Persephone, she did her best to resist but gave in and placed her hand in his. He drew her into the shower and closed the door, sealing them between glass and steam. Then he lifted her hand to his lips and kissed the backs of her fingers before placing her hand on his chest. His skin was hot, like the water pouring over his shoulders.

"Touch me, explore me. I'm yours," Roarke whispered. That low, hypnotic voice of his was irresistible. His dark, wet hair glistened like polished wood. She reached up to touch his face, tracing lines from his jaw to his ears, then down back his neck, lightly waking his skin with her nails. Exploring him was fascinating.

She'd never really felt she could touch a man like this and just *experience* him. He kept his hands on her hips, holding her, but letting her have the time to explore him without the distraction of him exploring her at the same time.

He let out a soft, drugged sound of pleasure, so she repeated the caress on the back of his neck. He was beautiful, *darkly* beautiful, and for the first time she felt, snowed in from the rest of the world, that she was free to have him all to herself. He lightly caressed her hips, and when she moved closer to him, her belly rubbed against his aroused cock. His fingertips dug tighter into her skin, and she realized he was struggling to control himself. Something about that made her feel strong in her femininity for the first time in her life.

"You really want me?" she asked as she traced his lips with the pad of her finger. He parted his lips, sucking the tip of her finger into his mouth. Then he flicked his tongue against the tip before nipping her lightly with his teeth. A bolt of fire shot between her thighs at that playful bite.

"I want you so bad it's killing me." His voice sounded gruffer now, an animal starting to show beneath his skin. She liked it, feeling the effect she had on him. So many other women she had known in her life loved to make men react, loved to be attractive and draw a man's desire. Shana had never wanted every man to want her. She just wanted one, the *right* one.

"If you want me, then take me," she urged him. A wildness built up inside her that she had been too afraid to embrace before now.

Roarke's lips quirked into a lazy grin. "Oh, I will, but I'm not rushing this, not with you, not when I've dreamed about this for years..."

He lowered his head and met her surprised inhalation by brushing his lips teasingly against hers, replacing her confusion over his words with prickling need, before he claimed her mouth fully and completely. He kissed her like the world was ending ... or perhaps beginning, as if the touch of their lips was the single most important thing in the universe ever to happen. She opened her mouth to his seeking tongue and moaned softly as he dueled his tongue with hers. Before she realized what was happening, her back met the cold plane of the glass shower. He leveraged her upwards, parting her knees with one of his so she sat riding his thigh, while he plundered her mouth. Her nipples tightened and her core ached for him to be inside her. He captured her wrists and pinned them against the cool marble on either side of her head while he held her up with a braced thigh.

Roarke kissed her deeply, decadently, wickedly, as he pressed deeper against her mound with his leg, rubbing his thigh against her clit which throbbed painfully. Breathy moans escaped her as she rocked herself against him while he kept her prisoner for his pleasure. She had never kissed a man like this before. As though she was created solely for pleasure, both hers and his. He mastered her easily, giving her almost enough to come apart but holding back just enough to torture her with need.

"Please, Roarke, I need you," she whispered between those intoxicating kisses of his.

"Do you, babe?" She hated and loved his playful whisper. "Tell me what you want me to do."

She wasn't used to vocalizing her fantasies. It was embarrassing and a little terrifying.

"I want you inside me," she whispered.

"Tell me details. I want to hear you say the words."

She couldn't say it. She wasn't a dirty talker except in her deep, dark fantasies. Even when she'd been with Jared, she hadn't been able to say what she wanted or needed during sex. But with Roarke, she thought maybe she could try.

"Come on, babe. I'm yours. It's just the two of us here, chase the ghosts of those past boyfriends away." Roarke nuzzled her ear and then bit the lobe tugging on it with his teeth. Fiery hunger forced words to her lips.

"Take control. Fuck me against the wall," she begged.

He moved his face away from hers to look at her, that sexy smirk making her knees tremble. It was a good thing she was straddling his thigh, or she might have collapsed.

"With pleasure, Shana, so much pleasure," he promised her. Then his mouth slanted over hers, kissing her hard, ruthlessly. It stole every thought from her, erased every worry. She could only feel, only experience, only bask in the rising lust within her.

He lifted her body up, cupping her ass cheeks as he pinned her higher up on the wall.

"Watch me fill you," he whispered gruffly. Then he adjusted her body and his before he pushed inside her hard and fast. The sudden pressure of him filling her completely made her gasp and throw her head back.

"Oh God..." she moaned as he sank fully into her, their hips slamming against each other's.

"That's it, babe. Take me deep, you feel fucking amazing," he growled as he withdrew and rammed back into her almost violently.

This was what she needed. A wild, frantic fucking that had no boundaries, no polite expectations. It was raw, unfiltered and rough, and everything she'd never had before but always hungered for. She opened her legs wider to take him deeper inside her. They set a driving rhythm which built and built until she couldn't take it anymore. She came so hard she saw stars and nearly blacked out screaming his name. Roarke kissed her neck and then bit her shoulder lightly as he hammered into her, and her skin absorbed his shout as he came.

For a second she clung to him, feeling adrift, lost in the vast sea of something new and frightening that had been unleashed inside her.

Roarke panted against her neck, his breath warm. The shower continue to spill hot water over their heated bodies. They were still in the shower, still pressed skin to skin in their own little private world. She never wanted to leave this small space so long as she was in his arms. She was undone ... unmade ... she could barely string a single coherent thought together.

"You okay?" he asked her after a moment. He was still inside her, still connected, and the intimacy of that after everything she'd felt toward him for years was strange.

"I ... yes." She tucked her head against his shoulder, secretly hiding her face from him as she came to terms with what she had just done.

She'd had sex with *Roarke Covington*, Chicago's resident bad boy lawyer. If her father knew, he would be furious. If Thad, Angelo and Jared knew, they would also be worried for her and pissed off at Roarke. What if—

"Hey, babe." Roarke lifted her head up with his hand and stroked her lips with his thumb. "Don't think, don't worry. Just feel, at least tonight."

How did he know what to say to her to calm the race of thoughts that sometimes shouted so loud in her head, it made her sick? He really was a dark prince casting his spell on her.

He kissed her forehead and then he slowly withdrew from her body, but he didn't let go of her as he lowered her back to her feet. She thought he would turn the shower off but instead he washed her, his hands gentle as he smoothed the lathering soap over her body. Emboldened by him, she did the same and washed him. She lathered his body, enjoying the feel of his muscles, the beautiful lines that formed his body, and she found it a calming experience like nothing else. To touch and be touched. To feel tenderness and to give tenderness to another person. She hadn't realized how lonely she had been until now.

Suddenly her eyes were burning with tears, and she was choking back a sob.

"Oh ... babe, come here." He pulled her flush against him, wrapping her tight in his arms.

"I'm sorry—" she hiccupped. "I'm not upset. I don't know why I'm crying," she tried to say between sobs. He gently fisted a hand in her hair at the nape of her neck so she couldn't look away from his eyes.

"Never apologize for what you feel when you're with me."

"It's just been so long since ... since anyone..." She didn't have the strength to finish. Roarke's eyes were deep and all-consuming as he looked at her.

"Let me love the lonely out of you," he murmured.

She nodded, desperate for him to continue to make her feel everything she'd not felt in years.

"For the next few days, you're mine, and for however long you want me after that. You don't ever have to feel lonely again, Shana."

In answer, she rocked up on her tiptoes and kissed him.

HE'D ALWAYS GUESSED THAT SHANA PIMMS WOULD BE THE death of him. He remembered the first day he ever saw her. He'd been sitting on the grass in front of the law library just enjoying the moment with no questioning professors, no endless pages of tort cases to read or brief. He was simply *in* the moment. His parents had hated that he'd chosen to go to Creighton's School of

Law. In Nebraska. Why would he ever want to go to a midwest school for farmers? Those had been his father's words. Roarke couldn't have explained his choice even if he wanted to.

Ever since he had met Thad, Angelo and Jared at prep school, he'd seen a different side of life. He'd seen loyal friendships and what a gift hard work and dedication to something could give a person. He wanted to be a part of their world, not the one he'd been born into. So he followed Jared to Creighton, despite knowing he would never really convince Jared to let him be a friend. Still, he had wanted to try, like a lonely kid who sees a happy family celebrating Christmas while he's on the outside, in the cold, looking into the window on a family he would never have.

One moment he was stretched out on the warm grass, and the next his world had tilted on its axis as Shana stepped out of the building just across the path from him. She had fucking *glowed*. There was no other word for it. The sun shone brighter down on her than anyone else. Hell, he was convinced he'd heard a choir of angels singing too, as she'd broken into a smile. She was heavenly.

He'd gotten to his feet, awestruck but determined to walk up to her and ask her out. But before he could reach her, she'd walked into the arms of another man who picked her up and spun her about, making her squeal before the man kissed her. When their lips parted and Roarke had a chance to see the man's face, his world had been overcast in instant shadows.

Of course she was *Jared's* girl. His hopes had crashed and burned in one epic freefall that had hardened his heart further, making him colder inside than he'd ever been before.

Three years... That was a long time to watch Shana and Jared break up and get back together over and over again. Each time, a glimmer of traitorous hope burned like a small ember in his chest as he sought Shana out, trying to make her give them a chance. But she never really saw him. It was like he was a ghost, a flickering image in the corner of her vision. She had only ever had eyes for one man, and that had never been him.

But right now, in this very moment ... he, not Jared, had Shana in his arms for the first time, and he hoped not for the last. His beautiful girl had been lonely. He had seen the ache in her eyes as she cried in his arms. She had damned near broken his heart with her tears. He had meant what he had said to her. He would love the lonely out of her. He would touch her, caress her, kiss her, make love to her over and over until she wasn't lonely anymore. She deserved to be with a man who worshiped her—but not from afar. Rather, she needed a man who would give anything to be a part of her life, the highs and the lows, the laughter and tears. He wasn't a hero; he wasn't a knight in shining armor. He was simply the man who had always loved her. He would likely never get the chance to tell her that, or even prove it to her, but he would take what few graciously granted days he could have with her.

He shut off the water and opened the shower door.

"Stay there," he told her and then retrieved two large, fluffy white bath towels from the rack above the toilet. He wrapped one around his waist, and then he unfolded the second one and held it up like a blanket to wrap around her as she stepped out of the shower. She turned her back to him and he wrapped it around her body and hugged her from behind.

"How..." Her voice still held a tiny, emotional hitch in it. "How are you this nice?" she asked in complete and total bafflement.

"I've always been this nice ... when it comes to you." He kissed her cheek. "Take your time in here. I'll change outside. Do you need anything from your bag?"

"Um... my pink cotton underwear and the silk PJ set on the top of my clothes when you open the suitcase."

"I'll get them," he assured her. Then he left the bathroom and found what she needed and placed them in her arms. She lifted her eyes up to meet his, and he fell into her blue gaze, dizzying in their depths. For such a quiet woman, she spoke volumes with those dazzling eyes. He wanted to spent the rest of his life discovering the mysteries in her.

"Thanks." Her cheeks turned red, and he smiled. They both knew she needed a minute to herself after what had happened between them in the shower.

She closed the door, and he stripped off his towel and threw on some pajama pants. He was towel drying his hair when she opened the bathroom door again. His eyes landed on her legs—beautiful, muscled legs that went on for days. He was a leg man, and Shana had the best legs. She wore pink and black polkadot silk shorts and a short sleeve button-up matching top. Her blonde hair, still damp, hung in burnished gold tendrils down her shoulders. She was adorable and sexy. He wanted to tumble her back into the bed and take her again, but he also wanted her to have a little space. Coming at her too strong and too fast wouldn't be good for either of them.

She lifted up her cell phone. "Should we text Jared about the other side not being able to get here for the meeting?"

"Yeah, I'll text him. Do you need anything?" He peeled back the sheets to his bed, and she tiptoed over to her bed and did the same.

"No, I think I'm good." She tucked herself beneath her sheets. He reached for his phone before he got into his own. He sent Jared and Thad a group text.

Roarke: *The other side of our deal was a no-show. They*

got snowed in at the airport in Berlin.

He had just set down the phone when it vibrated.

Thad: Seriously?

Roarke: Yep. Weather is bad here too, so Shana and I are stuck at least for another couple of days.

Jared: If you aren't a gentlemen, Covington...

Roarke chuckled before he replied.

Roarke: I'll be whatever Shana wants me to be.

"What are you telling them?" Shana asked.

He glanced over her. She lay down, her head propped in one hand as she watched him with no small amount of concern.

"I just told them that we would be here for a few more days. No need for us to rush home. Not me, anyway."

Her brows rose at that. "You don't have any Christmas plans?"

He set his phone down on the small nightstand between their two beds. "Nope. You?"

"Nope," she echoed. "My dad works practically every single day of the year and my mom ... she lives a life of her own. Dad and I aren't really a part of it."

"Sounds a lot like my family," Roarke said. He leaned back against the headboard and folded his arms behind his head.

"It kind of feels like we're at summer camp." Shana suddenly giggled.

"Oh yeah? Did you go to a lot of camps as a kid?" he asked, genuinely curious. He had never been to any. Rich kids went to prep schools, which were like worse versions of summer camps. Instead of a month of being picked on by other kids, it was a full year of torture from upper-class bullies.

"Once, when I was fourteen. A girl in our cabin snuck her boyfriend in. I had the bunkbed above them."

"Oh God, that sounds awkward." He turned on his side to face her.

She laughed. "It was. It really was. Thank God we don't have bunkbeds. I forgot I was on the top bunk and rolled off one night. It hurt like hell. I banged my knees and elbows."

"No shit," he chuckled. "Now I'm really glad we don't have bunkbeds. The only banging I want you to do is with me."

She laughed and threw one of her extra pillows at him. It was too easy to tease her, and he liked seeing her laugh.

"Ready for me to turn off the light?"

She nodded and he clicked the lamp on the nightstand off.

"Maybe tomorrow we could ... push the beds together?" she suggested in the dark.

Roarke grinned. "Yeah, maybe we could."

4

Shana stretched and yawned as she soaked in the warmth of the bright morning light that bathed her bed. Puzzled, she realized this didn't feel like *her* bed; it was softer than normal. Her body was sore—but it was a good kind of soreness. The kind a person got when they'd been active the day before, both out of bed and *in* bed. When she extended a bare leg out from beneath her fluffy covers, she remembered how she'd gotten so sore, and the heated memory tugged her lips into a smile.

A deep masculine chuckle had her eyes flying open.

Roarke Covington leaned against the wall opposite her twin bed in the Swiss hotel room they shared. Her cheeks flamed as she remembered *how much* they'd shared the previous night, and her belly flip-flopped at the deliciousness of it. Leveraging herself onto her elbows, she regarded the well-dressed man who stood before her: dark jeans and a black sweater that clung to his body and made her nipples pebble under her silk pajama shirt.

"Good morning, beautiful." He smiled at her and lifted a mug of coffee to his lips. The scent of an expensive dark roast drifted from the cup. It smelled divine.

She blushed with delight at being called beautiful because when Roarke said it, it meant something more meaningful than if any other man had called her beautiful. He wasn't just a man throwing out a pet name from habit. When he said the word, it seemed like he was really seeing her for who she was.

"How long have you been awake?" She delicately tucked her bare leg back beneath the covers.

"An hour. I brought you breakfast." He nodded at a tray that rested on the table between their beds.

"Thank you! That was nice." She scooted into a sitting position and reached for the tray. Breakfast in bed. She'd never had that before. The tray was laden with pastries and orange juice, as well as a bowl of oatmeal dusted with pecans and brown sugar.

"Is this a cherry?" she asked as she took a nibble of the Danish. Sweet cherries burst with delicious flavor on her tongue.

"I remember once that you said you liked them," Roarke said.

His admission warmed her, and she lifted her eyes from the gooey pastry to smile directly at him.

"I do." She licked her lips and took another bite before continuing to speak. "My grandfather loved Danishes. We always used to eat them together when I saw him on the holidays." She missed her grandfather. Her heart still hurt in the shape of his absence, feeling that emptiness he'd left behind. "He was my favorite person in the entire world."

Roarke pushed away from the wall and sat down on the edge of her bed.

"Why was he your favorite?"

"He was a lawyer too, but one of those classy old lawyers. He always wore a three-piece suit to court. He was the kind of man who opened doors for women out of respect. And he liked *me*. He didn't think I was a waste of time or a disappointment. When I told him I wanted to be a lawyer just like him, he spent a month teaching me how to read and brief cases before law school so I'd be prepared ahead of time."

Her throat tightened as she spoke. She never talked about her grandfather. And given the rocky relationship between him and her father, once he'd passed away, she'd had little time alone to grieve. Her father had pushed her straight into work, trumping her feelings and needs yet again for billable hours.

"Is he still..." Roarke asked.

"No. He passed away three years ago. My grandmother had been his whole world. She got Alzheimer's a few years before she died and she was ... lost."

Roarke scooted a little closer. "Lost?"

"When someone you love suffers from dementia or Alzheimer's, it's like the person they were gets lost somehow. We used to visit her, and I would sit there and hold her hand. She would look at me, her eyes just endlessly, wordlessly searching for answers. It hurt me, but seeing my grandfather with her ... it was like I'd seen a priceless vase shattered. You could collect all the pieces, but you can never put the vase back together the way it had once been." She paused, her voice breaking a little.

"He would play music for her on an old record player when he visited her in the memory ward. They used to love to dance. After she fell ill, they couldn't; she'd forgotten how. But he would sit there and hold her hand and speak softly, telling her about all the grand nights they'd shared together. He loved her so deeply that for three years his love was strong enough for the both of them, but one night she slipped quietly away, leaving him behind. I think he felt betrayed by his own heart, that it dared to keep beating after she was gone. He only made it a year before he followed her."

She'd never talked about this with anyone before. And as much as the words hurt to say, it felt therapeutic to talk about it with Roarke. He was a good listener.

"I'm sorry I never got to meet him." Roarke's reply was honest, which made the sting of talking about her grandfather's death hurt far less.

She wiped away a few stray tears and tried to smile. "He would've liked you. He had a soft spot for rebels."

"I'm a rebel?" Roarke chuckled.

She ate a few spoonfuls of oatmeal. "Oh yes, a total rebel. Considering who your family is and what they probably expected of you, you still went to a midwest law school. You work in Chicago and do things your way."

"And to hell with what anyone thinks," he added with a cocky grin.

"Exactly."

She finished off her cherry Danish and sipped her orange juice. "Did you eat anything?" She licked frosting off her fingers.

"I did, downstairs. I didn't want to wake you. You were sleeping so peacefully."

"Oh…" It would have been nice to have breakfast in bed with him, but she didn't say that. It might make her sound needy or silly.

He leaned in and brought her fingers to his lips. He sucked the remnants of the sweet frosting off her fingertips—and just like that, her body burned with fresh desire.

"Get dressed. Wear something warm that you can move in," he said as he got up off the bed.

"What? Why?"

"We are going to see a glacier."

"A glacier? They have one here?"

Roarke laughed. "Yes, they have one and an amazing winter park around it. We could go up there, do a few things, and then finish the evening with dinner at the Botta restaurant where we can watch the sunset."

"That sounds incredible." It also sounded intensely romantic, and Shana wasn't about to complain about that. She was starting to fall in love with him. It was strange, how easy it was to be with him. She didn't worry as much about things when she was with him, nor did she worry what he was thinking. But most importantly, she liked being with him, liked the person she was when she was with him. When she was with Roarke, it felt like the most real version of herself she'd been in a long time. That had to be mean something.

"I figured seeing the Alps like that would be more memorable than buying a postcard in the gift shop in town."

Shana hastily finished her breakfast, then got out of

bed and grabbed some winter clothes to change into in the bathroom. After combing the tangles out of her hair, she joined Roarke as he grabbed his wallet and coat. She was glad she'd bought a puffy, dark blue marshmallow coat to stay warm. He wore a hunter green winter coat and looked ready to explore.

"Ready?"

She tapped the toes of her winter boots together and grinned. "Let's go."

GLACIER 3000, THE WINTER PARK THAT OCCUPIED A SPACE on the top of a mountain, offered an amazing panoramic view of the Alps. Roarke had always wanted to go there, but it seemed odd to go alone. Something amazing like that should be shared with another person. Now he could take Shana. A boyish giddiness filled him as he escorted her toward the doors of the Alpine lift that would take them up the mountain.

They boarded the lift with a dozen other people by stepping into the enclosed box, made mostly of glass, that ferried people up and down the mountain. Shana leaned into him, clearly nervous about the height as the car moved up into the air along the cable. He wrapped an arm around her waist, the hold both comforting and exciting as their bodies pressed close. He loved the feel of her so near to him. They ascended the mountain, marveling at the whitecapped mountainsides and the valleys full of powdery snow. Occasionally they saw someone ski down the mountain below them. The skiers created wide arcing sprays of snow as they made turns going back and forth.

When the cable car reached the top, they exited and headed for a path that led to a suspension bridge.

"What's the Peak Walk?" Shana pointed to a sign as they made their way up the path.

"It's the only suspension bridge in the world that connects two mountain peaks."

"A bridge?" She paused at the end of the bridge and eyed the narrow path with clear anxiety.

"We're standing on View Point, the smaller of two peaks. That over there on the other side is Scex Rouge." He stepped out onto the bridge a few feet but stopped when he realized she hadn't followed him. He turned and looked back at her. She stood rooted a foot from where the bridge started, her posture rigid and her eyes wide with fear.

"I don't think I can cross that. I'm not good with heights," she admitted.

Roarke walked back to her. "I can see that," he murmured soothingly. He put himself between her and the bridge, blocking her view of it as he cupped her face. Her nose was turning red from the cold so he bent his head, nuzzling her in an Eskimo kiss. She relaxed against him, leaning in as their lips met in a slow, sultry kiss that almost made him forget where they were. He finally broke the kiss and savored the dreamy-eyed look she gave him. Her fear had been banished for a few brief moments. He felt a surge of pride mixed with relief and something else that he didn't dare name.

"I would never force you to do something you're not comfortable with. If you don't want to cross with me, I get it—it's scary. But the view is apparently worth the adrenaline. We'll be high above the clouds looking out at a snow-covered Swiss countryside. I promise the view is spectacular if, if you want to try it. I'll hold your hand the whole way, babe."

The look she gave him was one that he would never forget—an expression of complete and total trust as she held out her hand.

"You promise?" she asked.

"I promise."

He took her hand and for good measure put an arm around her waist. "Come on. We'll walk together side-by-side. It's only a hundred and seven meters. You can make it."

The first few steps out onto the bridge, she leaned heavily into him, and he took her weight, helping her feel like she was lightly stepping on the bridge. She stared down into the misty sky beneath them, her fingers digging into his gloved hand. Her breath escaped in little, panicked pants.

Shana's hands dug into his arm as she held on for dear life, but she kept moving and he moved with her, knowing she was stiff with fear, yet trusted him with every step she took. It humbled him beyond words to know this beautiful, brave, smart and compassionate woman was literally trusting him with her life. Even though he knew there was little danger on the bridge, he knew that her body believed it was threatened, and the fear in her was warning her to turn back, but she didn't. God, she was fucking glorious.

They moved together side-by-side across the bridge that spanned the two mountain peaks. He paused once in the middle of the bridge, and she tried to close her eyes. She wrapped her arms around his waist and held onto him for dear life.

"Don't look down, look up," he said. "See those peaks in the distance?" He pointed to the distant mountains ahead of them. She nodded. "Those are the Alps —the Matterhorn, Mont Blanc, Eiger, Mönch and Jungfrau."

"They're so beautiful," Shana breathed and smiled up at him. "I'm still terrified, but you're right—this was worth it." She peeped around a second longer and then pushed at his chest. "Okay, beauty moment taken. Let's get to the other side so I can get off the bridge, okay?"

Trying hard not laugh at her adorable expression of determination as she shoved him along, he put his arm back around her waist and they started walking far more briskly toward the other peak. She kept hold of his hand the entire way. Something warm and bright cocooned his heart, and he felt so happy he almost couldn't breathe for a second.

When they exited the bridge, they ended up at a safe viewing location at the top of Scex Rouge. Below them lay a thick blanket of clouds.

"You weren't kidding. We really are above the clouds." Shana leaned on the rail and peered down at the vast expanse of beautiful white below them, their shapes rippled like white velvet.

"It's just so beautiful," she murmured. Roarke took in the sight of her, the way her skin was flushed with excitement and how her eyes gleamed bright and her lips curved in a smile. He thought of how she'd braved the bridge to get here, and he was filled with such a bright and burning joy that he could scarcely stop himself from hauling her into his arms and kissing her senseless.

"It is beautiful," he agreed, but he had eyes only for her, always had. He didn't want to think about what it would be like when they went back to Chicago. She might retreat behind her protective friends and bury herself in work for her father, who would never value and appreciate her. And Roarke...would be left out in the cold again. Only this time it would be worse because he knew what he would be missing without her.

She turned to look up at him. "Thank you."

"For what?" he asked.

"For giving me a chance to just be myself and do something like this."

She stood up on her tiptoes and kissed him. It was a soft kiss, not one meant to seduce his body, yet it was a siren's call to ensnare his heart. He couldn't resist reaching up to cup her face in his hands and return the kiss. Last night they'd fucked like desperate animals, needing to be with each other on a primal level, but today was different. The kisses they'd shared today were softer, sweeter, yet no less passionate than last night. They held affection and trust, which somehow deepened the impact of the kisses on him.

"Roarke," she spoke softly. "Why do the others hate you so much?" she asked.

He almost smiled at the way she called Thad, Angelo and Jared "the others."

"Why?" he asked.

"Tell me here on this mountain. No one will hear, no one will..." She faltered.

"No one will judge?" He somehow sensed what she been about to say.

"Yeah, I guess that's what I meant."

He gazed at her a long moment, drinking in the sight of her. When a man like him looked at a woman he adored, like Shana, it was easy to become drunk on her beauty. He couldn't say no to her.

"The others never liked me because I was from a world that looked down on them," he admitted. "I'm old money from an old family. Being from that world comes with a price. They assumed they knew what sort of person I was, but—"

"They were wrong," Shana finished for him. "Why didn't you ever correct them?"

"I had a bit too much fun provoking them. I still do." He grinned at her, but she didn't laugh or smile back.

"Someday I'll make them see you the way you deserve to be seen."

He didn't doubt that she would try, and he loved her infinitely more because of it. He'd never said it even in his own mind before, but he loved her. He'd loved her that moment on the quad at Creighton when he'd seen her for the first time. He didn't care that it sounded like some sort of 'instant love' nonsense. For him, it was just the truth. And no one had the right to challenge what he felt in his own heart.

"Would you like a picture?" A middle-aged woman

was watching them on the platform. "I'll take one, if you want," she offered with a bright smile.

Roarke glanced at Shana. "I'd like to ... if you do."

"Yeah, I'd love that." She waved the woman over and handed over both her phone and Roarke's after he lifted it out of his coat pocket.

"Okay, lovebirds, give me a big smile," the woman said as she took a few photos. "Now turn and look at each other," she encouraged.

Roarke wrapped his arms around Shana and gazed down at her, unable to deny how happy he was in this moment. He pushed away the heavy stone of fear that weighed down his stomach at the thought of losing her.

"Got it!" The woman handed back their phones.

"Thank you," Roarke said.

The woman winked at him. "I remember how busy I was on my honeymoon. We forgot to take photos half the time."

Shana blushed but didn't correct the woman, and neither did he.

"Come on, let's cross back over the bridge. I have something else for us to do."

"Oh?" She looked a little apprehensive, which made him laugh out loud, the sound echoing off the distant tops of the Alps.

"Trust me, you'll love it. No more frightening heights, I promise."

"Good, I'm holding you to that. I've pushed my boundaries enough for one day."

He hoped she hadn't though, because tonight he wanted to make love to her again—and he didn't want either of them to feel like they had to hold back.

ROARKE WAS RIGHT. SHE DID LOVE WHAT HE HAD planned. She sat on a dogsled with him behind her, cushioning her so she could rest against him. The entire day felt strangely surreal and yet she had been memorizing every detail—from the bite of the cold to the crisp mountain air. Now, she had the warmth of Roarke's body behind her and the excitement of sled dogs in front of her. She didn't want to forget a single thing about today. Ahead of them, a team of huskies were barking and howling at each other in excitement.

"Are you ready?" their sled driver asked. He stood on the sled rails extended behind the back of the sled.

"Ready!" Shana and Roarke both said at once.

"Line out!" the driver shouted at the dogs in English. The huskies all moved to line up, their harnesses pulled taut as they leaned forward.

"Hike!" the man barked. The dogs leapt forward, the sled gliding smoothly behind them.

Roarke wrapped his arms around Shana, and she leaned back against him as the dogs tore off across the snow. They glided along a long circular path to view the entire glacier and the other beautiful scenery. The sled would carry them through the entire journey.

The glacier and the snow-dusted mountains around them glittered in the sunlight. The freshly churned, powdery snow glinted as though someone had cast a handful of diamond dust over everything. Shana had never seen snow so beautiful before. In Chicago, it often fell and turned immediately into gray slush on the streets. This, though, was like a fairy tale. She absorbed Roarke's warmth and his body steadied hers and she marveled at how perfectly they fit together, even in a dog sled. Everything about Roarke felt right, almost frighteningly so.

The huskies ran, their tongues out as they flashed dog smiles while they pulled the sled around the glacier park. When they finally returned to the beginning of the circular trail, Shana was truly sad the experience was over. She took her time petting each of the bright-eyed dogs who had given her such a fun ride. Each one had a different personality and look, and all of them were beautiful and sweet. She got more than one lick on her cheek, which made her giggle. When she was done, she noticed Roarke watching her.

"You really like dogs," he said.

"I do."

"But you don't have one." Roarke seemed puzzled by that.

"No. As you can imagine, my dad doesn't like unpredictable chaos. Pets are definitely that. Mom didn't want anything wrecking her perfect house. So the extent of what I was allowed were fish. Well, one fish—a beta fish. Even after all these years, I forget that I could have a dog now if I wanted, but given how much I work, the dog would be lonely."

"So you had a beta fish?"

"Yeah, you know ... one of those Japanese fighting fish. They have the long flowing tails in bold colors."

"Oh yeah, those the ones you can't put in the same tank."

"Just the males can't be together. You can't even really have them in tanks next to each other for too long either. They can exhaust themselves by puffing out their fins and challenging the other male while posturing. It is cool to watch them do it for a few minutes though. They really put on a show."

"Hmmm, sounds like males don't change their behavior much between species."

Shana couldn't resist laughing. "You're kind of right about that."

They said goodbye to the sled driver and his dogs before they started across the snow toward the restaurant at the top of the nearest hill.

"So, what was your fish's name?" Roarke reached for her hand while they walked, and she put her gloved palm in his.

"Sir Francis Ahab Drake." She laughed at the look on his face.

"That's a mouthful, isn't it?" Roarke grinned.

"I knew he was probably the only pet I could ever have so I named him twice, sort of."

"What do you mean you named him twice?"

"He's Ahab from Moby Dick, but he's also Sir Francis Drake, the Elizabethan era sea explorer."

"You are such a nerd," he said.

She elbowed him but giggled. "I am a nerd. But I own it."

"Good, because nerds are sexy," he said.

She inwardly shouted in triumph. "You think so?"

"Yeah, like I said, put on those glasses and tell me a book is due in your most bossy voice, and I'm yours forever, babe."

He was teasing, she knew that, but she pretended for a little while longer that he meant it.

They got to Botta just in time to watch the sunset

from the window seats. The setting sun formed a dark vermilion line on the horizon, blackening the once white Alps in a romantic silhouette. She'd never seen a thing like it in her life. It was a view only available on a mountain like this.

"Worth the climb?" Roarke asked as he held up his wineglass to her in a toast.

She lifted her glass and clinked it against his. "Worth every minute."

Shana remembered the heart-pounding fear of standing at the edge of the suspension bridge between the two peaks and how it felt to face the fear. She knew she would still be afraid of heights, even the same height if she had to cross the bridge again. But she had wanted to be with Roarke and to see the view from the peak on the other side, so she had mastered her fear, at least in that moment. And it had been worth it. *So worth it.* The best things in life were worth facing one's fear. She had known that once, long ago, but after her grandfather died she had lost sight of that.

Roarke had reminded her how to live.

5

"**I** have one more trick up my sleeve tonight," Roarke said as they arrived at the hotel after the sun had set.

"Oh?" Shana was exhausted, but she was also curious about what he had planned.

"Ahh, there it is." He grasped her by the shoulders and gently turned her away from the door of the hotel before she could go inside.

A beautiful red and gold sleigh came toward them on the road, with a team of Frieberger draft horses pulling it through the snow. A driver was perched in the front, but the rest of the sleigh was open for two people to sit in.

"We're going on a sleigh ride?" she asked as the horses stopped in front of the hotel.

"It's not too cliché, is it?" Roarke asked. A charming wrinkle formed between his brows, and he looked suddenly unsure of himself. Her heart melted completely. He would never know, and she would never tell him, but seeing how much he wanted her to like this and like him... *That* mattered more than anything else he could do.

"It's wonderful. I've never touched a horse, but I love them. And I had no idea anyone did sleigh rides except in movies."

Roarke chuckled, his body relaxing. "Come here. Let me introduce you to the horses."

She followed him down the steps of the hotel. The Frieberger horses were incredibly tall and thickly muscled, with glossy coats the color of molasses. The socks of their legs were white just above their hooves and they stood steady and calm as Shana came toward them.

"The horses are named Gold and Silver. Don't ask me to tell you the names in German or French; I couldn't pronounce them." Roarke removed his glove and gently but confidently ran his elegant masculine fingers down the nearest horse's nose. It huffed and bumped his hand in greeting.

"You want to try?" Roarke asked.

"Can I?" She removed her gloves hesitantly.

"Stroke him gently, but don't move too fast." Roarke

stood right behind her as she reached out and touched the horse. Its coat was soft, almost silky. The tip of his nose had a funny sort of fleshy texture that was also soft to the touch. She laughed when he bumped her hand like he hadn't Roarke's.

"They are beautiful," she breathed.

"Here is nobility without conceit, friendship without envy, beauty without vanity..." Roarke said.

"It's true, isn't it? They are strong, beautiful, with such a quiet nobility. It's humbling to stand before them." Shana leaned back against him, and he wrapped an arm around her from behind, holding her close. She could have stayed in his embrace forever.

"Let's sit down in the sleigh. I'm sure the horses are anxious to be off." He escorted her to the sleigh and they climbed in. A large, thick, faux fur blanket of pale gray lay on the seat and after she and Roarke sat down, he tucked them both beneath the blanket. Then he retrieved a pair of thermoses and handed her one.

"Hot chocolate," he said. "With Bailey's Irish cream."

"Oh God, that's my favorite."

"I know." He winked at her and then told the driver they were ready to go. The driver clicked his teeth and lips before gently tapping the horses' flanks with a flexible rod, and the sleigh began to move.

As Shana watched the landscape around her, she

wondered how long Roarke had been noticing her without her noticing him like that. He knew so much about her, her likes and dislikes, her passions. She'd been too busy mourning her breakup with Jared to notice anyone else like that, and it made her feel like a fool. If she'd only pulled her head out of the proverbial sand she would have seen Roarke in the shadows, waiting for her to notice him back. She burrowed closer to him and curled one arm around his stomach, savoring his warm, hard body beside her.

The sleigh toured through the town, which was blanketed with a fresh layer of snow. Merry lights twinkled from the roofs and hung across pedestrian shopping streets. Dozens of people filled the streets, stopping to buy presents and eat at restaurants. Shana liked seeing so many people have a wonderful time so close the holidays.

For a long while they didn't speak. She and Roarke simply enjoyed the clopping of the hooves and merry ring of sleigh bells. It was almost surreal, like living in some sort of dream. She'd thought she'd never find her prince charming, that a girlish dream like that was silly, but she realized princes did exist... Roarke was one of them.

Yes, he masked his charms to others with sarcasm and dark humor and enjoyed riling Jared and the others up a lot in business deals. But with her ... he was every inch the dream prince. He had only shown her compassion, affection, and care while they'd been here. It didn't feel like it was a game for him to be with her; he wasn't playing her while looking for his next conquest. This wasn't a façade that would fade. She felt that, deep inside, in a way she'd never been so sure of anything else in her life.

"So what about you?" she asked, going back to their earlier conversation. "Are you a pets-and-kids kind of guy, or a bachelor with dozens of women in dozens of cities waiting for you to visit?" She was trying to tease him, but he didn't smile. She honestly didn't think he had a dozen women in different cities, but she wanted to see if she could get him to blush the way he was always making her.

"I would actually love pets and children, but not with just anyone. When I tie my life to someone else's, it won't be done casually. I don't want to be like my parents. I won't marry old money or for social reasons. No marrying a woman for her looks or how she is in bed. I want a woman to want me and a life with me, without a thought to money or social connections. If she doesn't want me, then it's not meant to be. I want a partner in life and love."

Shana held her breath as she absorbed his words. "Would you get up at one a.m. to feed a crying baby or change a diaper?" she asked. She remembered how tired Felicity and Jared were after Hayley was born, but somehow, being in that moment together, the two of them as parents were united in their love for their child and both working to help each other. It had deepened their love.

It was probably a bad idea to throw such a serious question at Roarke, but if she got in any deeper with how she felt about him, she'd want everything with him, the good and the bad. And she had to know… What kind of man was he when it came to the hard stuff? She knew he was the perfect romantic, but how would he handle the tough nights?

"Yes," he answered, "and I would go to every birthing class with my wife. We would be partners. I'm not my father, and I refuse to have his or my mother's marital or parenting failings." He finally met her gaze. "What about you?"

"I want the same as you. I want to be a mother, but I want to keep working too. I want a husband who is involved in all aspects of my life and treats me with respect and values me as a human being. I want to be equal parents with equal responsibilities."

"You have every right to ask that and more of any man who marries you," he assured her as he pulled her a little closer to him.

They grew quiet again, watching the stars above flickering, winking in the velvety black sky.

"Why did you and Jared break up so often and get back together all the time while we were in law school?" Roarke's question caught her off guard.

"You noticed that?" During law school, she'd never thought Roarke so much as looked at her except when they were in study groups preparing for finals. He had kept to himself so much during those three years of school. They'd chatted politely during this study sessions, but she hadn't thought he'd paid attention to her much beyond that.

"Of course I did," he said quietly.

Shana finished her hot chocolate and realized the Bailey's Irish creme was making her more honest and emotional than she usually was about things like this.

"I think he loved the idea of me, not the reality of me, and I ... I just wanted to be loved so I didn't care. It's so cliché—the girl who had no love growing up looks for it in every man she dates." Tears gathered thickly on her lashes, and she hastily wiped them away.

"Wanting love when you've been given none is not cliché. It's human." Roarke put an arm around her shoulders and tucked her against his side again.

In that moment, Shana wished it had been Roarke she had met first. If she had ... she might have had a different life, a life not burdened with a complicated romantic past which had led to a lonely life. She stared at Roarke's mouth and then curled her hand in his sweater to pull his head down to hers.

The kiss burned deliciously, but it was also bittersweet. She could almost taste the life she might have had if only she had met Roarke instead of Jared first.

Was it too late to change her future? Could she and Roarke make something lasting out of the fire that burned between them?

Their mouths parted, and he rested his forehead against hers. She still had her fingers curled in his sweater, and she breathed in the natural scent of him, mixed with the slightest hint of cologne. She was beginning to learn Roarke did a lot of things to perfection, right down to not overdoing the amount of scent he used. He seemed to exercise limitless control over himself and his environment. What would happen if he lost control of himself and his world? Would he crumble? Would he break? She had so little control of so much that she felt on the verge of breaking all the time.

"What are you thinking?" he asked her.

She dared not tell him.

"So, are you a cat or a dog person?"

He closed his eyes and laughed softly. "Such deep concentration for such a simple question."

"Well? Which is it? Cats or dogs?"

"I really like cats, but I would love a dog. There was a golden retriever that lived next door to me when I was a kid. His name was Zeus. He sort of adopted me and seemed to sense how lonely I was."

"Zeus?"

"Yeah, like the Greek God." Roarke grinned, the boyish expression utterly charming. "He was a brave dog and whenever it stormed, he would always come and sit on the porch with me and watch the lightning streak across the sky. I guess his owners knew that he wasn't afraid of storms, hence his name."

For a moment she pictured the cute little boy he must have been huddled on a porch, his arm around a golden retriever while they watched a thunderstorm. He must have been so lonely, feeling lost in that cavern where his parents' love should have been.

"Are you familiar with Greek mythology?" She'd always been interested in mythology, but she'd never really talked to anyone else who was too.

"Yeah, I am. I wasn't a typical middle schooler. My father made a snide comment about my lack of reading one summer so I grabbed the fattest book I could find, which happened to be a huge book of Greek mythology tales. I didn't think I'd like it, but I wanted to prove him wrong." Roarke smiled bashfully. "It was interesting. I realized I enjoyed reading it more than I thought I would."

"Do you still read? Most lawyers lose their love of reading during law school." She found she was fascinated by him, and wanted to know everything about him, the way he seemed to know so much about her.

"I think I read more now than I did in law school," he remarked with a note of self-curiosity. "I remember a lot of our classmates saying that they couldn't stand to read once they'd finished reading cases. I never got that. Reading an esoteric constitutional law case is completely different than opening up a suspense thriller."

"Or a romance novel," she added. "Those are my favorite."

"I'm not surprised." He tapped the tip of her nose playfully with his index finger.

"Is that because I'm a woman or—"

He silenced her with a gently placed finger over her lips. "Because you're hopelessly romantic, and that's not because you're a woman; that's just because you're you." Then he removed his finger and leaned in, replacing it with his lips, and she sighed in contentment at his kiss. He was so good at it. Jared had been a wonderful kisser, but he never kissed her with the intensity and reverence that Roarke was showing now. He had a relaxed intensity that left Shana feeling dizzy and aroused all at once.

She wasn't sure how long they kissed while the sleigh moved through the snowy night. The horses' harness jingled with bells in a merry, musical way that made Shana feel she was in a place out of time, a realm of magic and wonder. With bells ringing and the smell of baked chestnuts and chocolate being sold on street corners, mixed with the laughter of children chasing each other along the walking paths while throwing snowballs, it all felt so wonderfully cozy. Like the front of a Christmas card.

Shana used to love Christmas cards, seeing the frosted landscapes and the people living out a wonderful holiday. She'd grown up and discovered that holidays weren't like that... Or so she'd thought. Here she was living a Christmas card dream with Roarke and it was real, every minute of it.

But even magic had to end. Finally, they were back in the front of their hotel and it was time to bid the horses goodbye. They thanked their driver, and he held out sugar cubes, which she and Roarke offered to the horses. Shana couldn't help but laugh when one of the Clydesdales licked her palm while scooping the sugar cube out.

Then they waved at the driver before the sleigh vanished into the night.

"You know..." she said in a whisper so she didn't disturb the peaceful snowy evening, "I think you might be a romantic too."

"With you ... I certainly am." He didn't even try to deny it, and that made her feel warm all over.

When they went inside, the hotel was full of people and she recognized a wedding party that had been there when she first checked in. A bride stood in a flowing white gown, greeting people in the lobby. Shana watched with an earnest longing when she saw how the groom and bride shot secretive, loving looks at each other.

"Envious?" Roarke asked.

"No, not envious. I just love how happy they seem."

"Would you ever do a big wedding?" he asked her.

"No, I don't think so. Something small and private. Something for just my family and close friends. I thought maybe a destination wedding to Scotland would be fun."

"Would your groom have to wear a kilt?" Roarke asked with a smile.

"No, unless he wanted to." She winked at him, and he put an arm around her shoulder.

They carefully worked their way through the guests in the crowd before she stopped to look at him.

"I forgot!" She pulled away from him and rushed back toward the front desk. She was done speaking to the woman there by the time Roarke reached her.

"Everything okay?" he asked.

"Yeah, I just remembered. The twin beds."

"What about them?"

She tilted her head slightly and shot him what she hoped was a seductive look as she leaned in to whisper.

"We need them pushed together, remember?"

"Yes, we do, don't we?" He seemed pleased at the request and she grinned. "Let's have a drink at the bar before we go up. That will give them time to take care of our room."

They took a seat at the bar and ordered two glasses of wine. Shana was feeling rather good after the little bit of Bailey's Irish cream in her hot chocolate, but one glass of wine would remove the last of her worries tonight. She wanted to seduce Roarke. She wanted to show him she wasn't a princess on a pedestal, that she had hungers and desires that matched his own.

She would enjoy being with him while she could.

SHANA WAS UP TO SOMETHING, BUT ROARKE WASN'T SURE what. They sat at the bar and had drinks with another couple. The man was named Zeno Villani, the woman Chloe Taylor. Roarke felt like he'd heard of the Villani family, and their reputation was a bit iffy, but he liked Zeno. The man was sarcastic and cocky and had no filter whatsoever. Roarke didn't mind at all when someone was unapologetically themselves without worrying about what others thought.

Chloe was sweet, a college kid with big dreams to be a social media influencer. They were an odd pair together, but Roarke felt like they worked somehow. Not that Zeno or Chloe seemed to be aware of their growing attraction to each other. It amused Roarke. He was good at reading people, their faces, their bodies, their voices. It was what made him a successful lawyer. These two had it bad for each other and were only just starting to realize it.

"So, what brings you guys here to Switzerland?" Shana asked the couple while she sipped her wine.

"A wedding," they both said the same time and laughed. Zeno's green eyes sparkled as he glanced at the petite blonde beside him.

"I'm the maid of honor and Zeno is the best man," Chloe explained.

"Aww." Shana smiled. "How fun."

"It is," Chloe said and shot a shy glance at Zeno. "What about you guys? Honeymoon?"

Shana choked on her wine. "Oh, no, no... Roarke and I are business associates. We were supposed to be doing a business deal, but the other side we were supposed to meet with got stuck in Berlin."

"Business associates?" Zeno raised his dark brows as he looked to Roarke for confirmation.

"And friends..." Roarke gave a playful tug on a lock of Shana's hair. "We used to be enemies," he added, teasing her with a wink.

Shana blushed and rushed to correct him. "No we weren't, not really."

"She just dated my worst enemy," Roarke said.

Before Shana could protest this, Zeno added, "That's fucking hot." Zeno sipped his beer and shot Roarke a knowing grin.

A group of people walked past the bar. Spotting Zeno and Chloe, they shouted at the two to join them.

"Oh, that's the rest of our wedding party. We've got to run. Nice to meet you guys!" Chloe hugged Shana and beamed at Roarke before dashing off to grab the bride's arm and walk away with her. Zeno nodded at Roarke and Shana before heading in the direction of the remaining people waiting for them.

Shana glared at Roarke when they were alone. "We aren't enemies. We were never enemies."

"But imagine if we were," Roarke leaned in to whisper. "Imagine you and me facing off over a boardroom table ... negotiations getting heated, clothes getting ripped off next. We would fuck each other to within an inch of our lives..."

Her eyes dilated, and he knew she was imagining what he'd said.

"Or ... after work you sneak over to my apartment,

and I take you on every flat surface we can find all night long. Can you imagine that?"

Shana gulped down the last of her wine, set the glass on the counter and fixed him with a hot and desperate look that made him hard as nails. He was forced to adjust his pants before he stood up.

"Let's go upstairs. Now," she ordered. He finished his drink with a chuckle and followed behind her so he could watch her cute butt as she walked ahead of him toward the elevators.

The second the elevator doors closed on them, he moved. Roarke pushed Shana back against the wall and pinned her arms above her head while he kissed her hard. She moaned as he claimed her mouth roughly. She drove him insane like no other woman in his life ever had or ever would.

Shana tasted like a dream. She was fire and sweetness, and it made him desperate to be inside her again, to feel her pulse around him and join herself to him in a way that could never be undone. Roarke wanted to mark her, to own her and possess her, but he knew he never would. She was as free as a falcon riding the winds. He was but a humble man on the ground, gifted with the vision of watching her fly.

He reached over and hit the stop button on the panel. The elevator slowed to a pause between floors.

"What are you—" she began.

He didn't give her time to think, to question. He turned her to face the wall.

"Keep your hands on the wall," he ordered in her ear and she obeyed. It only made the hunger in his veins burn hotter. He unfastened her jeans and jerked them down her hips along with her silk panties, then he unfastened his own jeans and shoved them down enough to free his cock. With one hand he pulled her hips back toward him, and with his other hand he guided himself into her from behind.

"Oh..." Shana let out a soft sound of surprise, which turned it into a drugged sound of pleasure as he sank deep into her. It took him three thrust before he was fully seated inside her.

"Roarke..." She gasped as he moved one hand around her body to gently feather a fingertip over her clit. She jerked at the touch. He smiled at her sensitivity.

"Please..." she begged, pushing her ass back into his hips, encouraging him.

"Fast and hard now, slow later," he warned.

"Yeah..." she agreed.

He curled his fingers around the back of her neck, holding her in place, and then he fucked her hard. Each slam of his hips against her ass made her cry out in pleasure. She was tight and hot and wonderfully wet. He never wanted it to end. Making love to her was like seeing and touching heaven... It was an ephemeral moment of sheer, raw and glorious pleasure. It was brief, too brief. He wanted to be forever with her like this.

Roarke felt the second she came; her channel gripped him and he closed his eyes, feeling pure pleasure as he followed her over the edge. Shana gasped, bracing herself against the wall of the elevator. He leaned in and brushed the hair back from her neck before he kissed her.

"I think you broke me..." she whispered.

He curled an arm around her waist, holding her to him. "Are you hurt? Was I too rough?" He had never hurt any partner before, but he had lost himself in her like he never done before.

"I hurt ... but it's a good hurt. If I walk funny tomorrow, it's entirely your fault." She smiled at him over her shoulder, and in that moment he knew he was lost forever to this woman. He was still buried deep in her body, and she was teasing him. It was wonderful. It was intimate, sweet, and something else he couldn't quite name. He reluctantly pulled out of her and used a handkerchief to clean her and himself, and they did their best to straighten her clothes before he released the stop button. The elevator went up to their floor and the doors opened. An older couple stood there, looking unamused at the delay.

"See, Carl, it was coming. It was stuck," the woman said and walked past Shana and Roarke as they stepped out.

"Oh, it was *coming* all right," Roarke murmured with a wicked grin as he put an arm around Shana's shoulder. She gasped, her face turning red as a cherry, and she ducked her head until the elevator doors closed behind the couple.

"You are shameless," she said with a laugh as they reached their room.

"Life's too short to be ashamed." He had once carried shame; it was a part of his old life. But when he had gone to prep school and saw that he could leave emotion behind, he had done it gladly. Even if men like Thad and Jared still didn't trust him, he didn't carry that weight on his shoulders anymore.

He removed his key card and opened the door. The hotel employee was finishing the merging of the two twin beds into one large bed.

"Pardon me, I'll be done in just a moment," the hotel employee said as he finished tucking in the sheets on their new bed.

"No problem," Roarke said as the man fluffed a few pillows and then headed for the door.

"Thank you," Shana said to him.

"You're welcome! Enjoy your honeymoon."

When the door closed behind him, Roarke burst out laughing.

"Oh my God, he knows we're sleeping together."

"Yes he does, and he thinks we're married." Roarke pulled her into his arms and pressed a kiss to her forehead. She was so delightfully easy to embarrass.

"You want to shower?" he asked.

She nodded again with another blush. "You'd better join me."

"I wouldn't miss it." Roarke pulled her close to him and kissed her deeply, letting her think on all the things they might do tonight before he let her go.

This time he enjoyed the shower a lot longer than he had the previous time. Their lovemaking this time was pure, simple, and somehow tender. He sat down on the marble bench of the back of the shower and pulled her down onto his lap so that she straddled him. Then he kissed her long and slow, enjoying her mouth and the feel of her weight on his lap.

"Did you enjoy today?" he asked as he threaded his fingertips through her soaked hair. It felt silky against his skin.

Shana's soft smile wrapped around his heart and clenched it.

"I did. We did so much, it was like living a lifetime in one day." She curled her arms around his neck and pressed against him. He held her, happy to enjoy her embrace and nothing more. It was so clear she needed to be touched, to be loved, and hadn't been in a long time. His soul wanted to howl at such unfairness. She trembled a little, as if she sensed his thoughts, and kissed his neck.

"Why are you so good to me, Roarke? I'm not worth—"

"You are worth it, babe. More than you'll ever know." He rubbed his hands along her back, tracing the faint, delicate bones of her spine that led down to the curves of her hips and bottom.

"Roarke?" she murmured.

"Yes?" He could have done that all day, just touching and holding her. She was a drug, and he was a happy addict.

"Make love to me." She lifted her hips up, which brought her full breasts tantalizingly close to his mouth. He had never been one to refuse temptation, so he captured one nipple between his lips and sucked. She let out a soft gasp of sensual delight, so he sucked harder. When he tortured one nipple enough, he kissed a path across her chest to the other peak and wrapped his lips around it, pulling on it with his teeth, careful not to hurt her.

"Holy shit... Roarke." She dug her hands in his hair and tugged hard on the strands. The hint of pain shot from his scalp down to his shaft, and he groaned low at the back of his throat. He cupped her bottom and lifted her high until she could take his cock in her hand and guide him into her. The feel of her hand around him was almost as good as her body when he sank inside.

The sensation of being connected to her, holding her, was almost too good. A sudden lump of emotion caught in his throat, and he fought to control himself. They moved together, rocking slowly, their passion building and finally cresting, and in its wake came such an intense wave of tenderness. He felt raw inside, like every emotion he had ever buried in his life had been unearthed. It felt amazing and terrifying all at the same time. He searched her face and saw the same wonderment in Shana's eyes.

"That was something else, wasn't it?" she whispered.

"Yeah," he agreed. "You okay?"

She smiled. "You keep asking me that like I'm going to break."

"I can get carried away, and the last thing I want is to hurt you."

Her eyes softened and she traced his lips with a fingertip. "You are so sweet. I love that about you."

Roarke's heart constricted. Had she realized what she just said? Had she meant it more deeply than just as a passing comment?

They sat beneath the spray until Shana giggled at their pruned fingers. When he examined her hand, he gently took one of her fingers between his lips and sucked on it until she was gazing at him with new hunger, and he had to claim her all over again. This time he let her ride him facing away from him, and he'd never been so glad for a marble bench in a shower before in his entire life.

"We'd better go to bed," she said and stifled a yawn. "I'm dead after everything we did today."

Roarke agreed. Even though he was incredibly fit, hiking a mountain, walking the length of the glacier and several bouts of sex had him ready to crash too. But he felt good; he felt happy and satisfied in every way and he hoped she did too. She deserved to feel that way even more than he did.

They both dried off and got into their pajamas before they climbed into their now spacious full bed. They lay not touching for a long moment after he turned off the light, then Shana rolled over in the darkness and kissed his cheek.

"Night," she whispered as she settled into his body and stretched an arm over his stomach as if they'd slept that way together for years.

"Night," he echoed back.

As he fell asleep, he was still smiling.

6

The sound of a cell phone ringing woke Shana up from a cozy dream about sleigh rides and drinks by the fire. Their bodies were still tangled from last night, the heavy weight of his arm around her back and her leg tucked between his larger ones. She was curled up against Roarke, and he stirred as she sat up.

"Is that your phone or mine?" he asked drowsily.

"Mine, I think." She slid out of bed and retrieved her phone off her nightstand. She winced when she saw the time. It was a little after four a.m. Jared's name flashed across the screen.

"Hello?" She answered quietly even though Roarke was half awake. She felt bad disturbing him.

"Hey." The tone of Jared's voice was tense, and she

heard in it an underlying bleakness that filled her with fear. "Sorry, I know it's early for you, but I knew you would want me to call you."

"What is it?" she asked. Roarke stirred behind her, seeming to pick up on her worry.

"It's Angelo. He's in the hospital."

"What?" For a second, Jared's words made no sense.

"He's in bad shape, Shana. Is there any way you can get home in the next day or so?"

Angelo was hurt? Finally the words punched through her weariness and into her chest. Something had happened to one of her best friends. Oh god... She had to get home.

She nearly choked when she spoke next.

"What happened?"

"He was cooking in the soup kitchens like he always does on Christmas Eve, and a man attacked one of the workers when he tried to steal her purse. Angelo fought the guy off, but he was stabbed. You need to come home."

As Shana tried to process all of that, she was vaguely aware of Roarke getting dressed behind her.

Angelo was different than Thad or Jared. There was such an innate sweetness to him that made everyone adore him. It didn't hurt that he looked like a Greek god. Angelo had always looked out for her, especially when she and Jared had finally broken up once and for all. They'd spent a lot of time together, just as friends. She didn't want to think of Angelo hurting. He was always so strong. It was hard to picture him lying in a hospital bed, fighting for his life.

"I'll try to find the next flight out."

"Send me a text when you have flight details. Thad is at Disney with Veronica, and I can't reach him. He was planning to propose to her, so his phone is off. I left him a voicemail. I'm at the hospital with Angelo's family."

"Okay, I will. Thanks, Jared." She hung up and turned to Roarke. "Angelo is in the hospital. It's bad."

He raked a hand through his hair, his face solemn, his eyes shadowed. "What can I do to help?"

"I need to get a flight to Chicago as soon as I can."

"It's Christmas Day. I'm not sure how many options we have. Let me make a few calls. Give me your passport, and you can pack while I try to find a flight for us."

She rushed over to her purse and dug through the contents to find her passport. Her hands were shaking violently as she handed it to him.

He gently grasped her shoulders. "It's going to be okay. I'll find us a way to get home. I promise." Then he stepped into the hall and was gone for half an hour, which gave her the time to change into traveling clothes and pack up her suitcase and toiletries.

When Roarke returned, he pulled her into his arms

without even asking. It was as though he knew what she needed. She felt safe and protected in his arms, at least for a few moments while she could calm down enough to breathe.

"I called in a favor. I have a private plane that can leave in two hours. We have an SUV waiting for us downstairs that can drive us through the snow to the airport."

"Oh, thank God." She hugged him, burying her face against his chest and drew in a shuddering breath before she forced herself to let go of him. They had to get to the airport.

They packed the rest of their things and left the cozy retreat. As they rode in the back of the SUV to the airport, she sent Jared and Thad a group text with her flight details. Her phone connection was spotty halfway through the airport, and she was cut off from knowing how Angelo was doing.

She held onto Roarke's arm and pressed her face against his shoulder as she stared bleakly out at the snowy landscape. When they reached the airport and got through security, she turned her phone off and ignored the hungry growl of her stomach. Despite being hungry, she didn't think she could eat if she tried. She felt completely hollow as worry ate away at her.

Shana was not fully paying attention to anything as they boarded the private plane an hour later and took off. She and Roarke barely spoke on the flight, but he stayed close to her, giving her the silent comfort she needed of his presence. Her thoughts were drawn inward, on Angelo, and how she hated not knowing for the next nine hours if he was going to be okay.

At some point in the flight, exhaustion won out and she fell asleep against Roarke's shoulder. She woke when he gently shook her so they could exit the plane. Roarke had a private car waiting, and his driver took them straight to the hospital. It was a little after nine in the morning. When she checked her phone after turning it on, she saw Jared had told her Angelo was still at the hospital and in surgery, but that he'd been out soon and they'd know more about his condition by the time she arrived.

When she and Roarke got to the waiting room, she found Jared sitting beside Angelo's parents and older brother and sister-in-law. She rushed to hug her friends and then Angelo's family. Roarke lingered at the edge of the crowd and when she glanced his way, he gave her a reassuring nod as if to say he wouldn't leave.

"What's the latest news?" Shana asked Jared softly.

"He was stabbed only once but pretty deeply. The surgeon just told us he came through the surgery well and he's going to be okay. He'll be able to have visitors once he's awake. It may be another hour or so before he comes around."

Shana noticed a young red-haired woman in an oversized sweater curled up in the corner of the waiting room, watching them with sorrowful eyes.

"That's Kara. She's the woman Angelo rescued," Jared said. "She's the one who called 911 and got him here in time." Jared's voice broke a little on those last few words.

Shana knew how much Jared loved Angelo. He, Thad and Angelo were brothers in every way but blood.

Drawing upon what inner emotional strength she had left, she did her best to reassure Jared. "Angelo is tough. He'll pull through and be back at his restaurant, cooking, in no time." Shana kissed Jared's cheek. "Where are Felicity and Hayley?" she asked. She hadn't texted Felicity on the way home, not wanting to disturb her and their one-year-old baby.

"At home. I didn't want them here watching everyone stress over this. Hayley is at that age where she cries if she sees other people cry." He smiled a little, but his expression was sad.

"That's a good idea to leave them at home." Shana knew he should also be at home. Sitting here and worrying about Angelo wasn't the way Angelo would want him to spend Christmas. She turned her focus on Angelo's family. "Jared, you should go home. You have a family and it's Christmas. I'll call you when Angelo's awake. Thad and Veronica will be on a flight home tomorrow morning. It was the earliest they could manage."

Jared thought it over for a moment, and she knew he was weighing it in his mind.

"Seriously, Jared. You've been here all night. I'll take over for at least half the day. At least go home and shower."

"Okay, call me the minute he's awake."

"I will," she promised.

Shana, still exhausted, settled in a chair to wait for her friend to wake up. She had no family, not really. Her father would be working, and her mother would be in the Hamptons with her friends. Shana's only real family was here in this hospital. And that included Roarke now. He'd done more for her in the last twenty-four hours when she'd needed him most than anyone else had in her entire life. The thought warmed away the cold chill of the hospital's waiting room. She looked his way and smiled at him, and he smiled back. They were in this...whatever *this* was...together, she was sure of it.

ROARKE FELT HELPLESS. HIS WOMAN WAS HURTING, AND he had no way of helping her. The entire plane ride from Switzerland to Chicago, he'd kept a vigil over her, giving her anything she needed, even space and silence. Yet every minute that ticked away since they'd returned, he felt that happy bubble they'd created in Gstaad fading more and more beneath the weight of reality. She could turn away from him again, go back to the safety of her trio of protectors and hide from what he was offering her.

A smart man would have prepared himself better for whatever was coming next, good or bad, but Roarke wasn't ready. He only knew he was completely, irrevocably in love with Shana. He'd do whatever she needed, for as long as she needed him to. He just wished ... he wished for a lot of things he knew he didn't deserve. And that was always his problem, wanting things he couldn't have ... like the woman of his dreams. Still, for just a while longer though, he could pretend he had her. The way she'd smiled at him just now fed that foolish hope.

He watched from the corner of the room when she hugged Jared and then embraced Angelo's family members one by one. A pang of longing stung his heart as she kissed Jared's cheek and then sat down to wait. She flashed him another relieved, comforted smile and he couldn't help but smile back.

I'm here for you. Whatever you need, I'll get it for you, he silently vowed.Jared collected his coat from off the back of a nearby chair and came toward Roarke, who hovered in the waiting room doorway.

"Can we talk outside?" Jared asked.

"Sure." Roarke and Jared both left the waiting room to stand in the hallway outside. They stared at each other a long moment.

"Thank you for bringing Shana home," Jared said finally. "I'm sure it took a lot to find someone to fly you guys back on Christmas."

"It did, but I didn't mind calling in that favor," Roarke said. His gaze strayed to the waiting room door.

When he looked back at Jared, the man was frowning.

"What happened in Switzerland?" Jared asked.

"Nothing. The meeting was canceled, and we just hung out a little bit," Roarke reminded him, even though they both knew Jared didn't really mean to ask about the meeting.

"I meant between you and Shana."

"Nothing that concerns you," Roarke warned. He didn't want to hear a lecture on how to treat Shana from the man who'd had a yo-yo like dating history with her before he'd finally settled down with his soul mate, Felicity.

"Shana concerns me, Roarke, you know that. I want what's best for her. She's a wonderful person, and she's been through hell most of her life." He dragged a hand through his hair, and Roarke saw how tired the man was. He looked beaten down, worried sick over his best friend Angelo, and now he was worrying about Shana.

Roarke leaned against the wall and crossed his arms. A few nurses bustled passed them wearing Santa hats. They were most likely on their way to the children's wing. The thought pricked Roarke's heart with a quiet sorrow at the thought. Once the nurses were gone, Roarke spoke.

"What's best for Shana is ditching her job at her father's firm and leaving that toxic shit behind. What's also best for her is to not cling to the past she had with you."

"After I met Felicity, Shana and I never... We were done long before I met Felicity..."

"I know you never did anything. But Shana is still feeling the loss of the only semi-decent relationship she's ever had. And no other man in her life who should give a damn about her seems to care that she's *drowning*." His voice roughened on the word as he felt the strain of his worry over Shana suddenly overcome him. He was pissed and anxious because he knew what the drowning feeling felt like. "She deserves to be with someone who puts her first, someone who values all of her, the real her, not some boyhood fantasy of her. She's so much more than that. She deserves a partner in life that she can lean on and rely on."

Jared's eyes widened ever so slightly. "You're really in love with her." He gave a little shake of head. "Thad always said you liked her, but I didn't think it went deep."

"Of course I'm in love with her." He didn't deny it. "I fell in love with her the moment I saw her by the law library, but before I could tell her that, I watched her walk right into your arms." He drew in a slow breath to calm his suddenly racing heart. "It's always been her for me. No one's ever come close and until now ... I've never stood a chance with her."

Understanding softened Jared's face. "Does she know?"

"That I'd do anything for her?"

Jared nodded.

Roarke rubbed a hand along his jaw, trying to wipe away his weariness. He hadn't slept at all on the plane, in case she'd needed him. "I've tried to show her, but she's had a lot to worry about lately. I didn't want to add to that, by complicating her life with my feelings."

For a moment, neither of them said a thing. Then Jared sighed heavily.

"If you really care about her that much, don't miss your chance," he said. "Some people only get one shot at love. You might not get a second chance, so don't miss it. By the way... Love, real love, is never a burden, nor a complication."

"Are you giving me your blessing?" Roarke asked.

"Yeah, I guess I am, not that either of you need it." Jared suddenly smiled and clapped Roarke on the shoulder. "You just proved today you're not the asshole I always thought you were. That seems to be the second Christmas miracle I've had today after Angelo getting through surgery. Don't fuck this up, Covington. Marry her and give her the life she deserves."

"I plan to, if she'll have me," Roarke promised.

After Jared left, Roarke visited the hospital cafeteria and ordered a round of hot chocolates for everyone in the waiting room. He also insisted on running to a favorite restaurant of Angelo's mother and bringing back food for everyone. As he passed out the to-go containers, he felt Shana's eyes on him. He offered her a soft smile and their gazes met across the room.

She mouthed the words *thank you*, and he merely nodded in return.

WHEN SHANA HAD HER CHANCE, SHE ASKED ROARKE TO come with her to Angelo's room. He took her hand in his, and they went to see him together. When she entered the hospital room, she squeezed Roarke's hand tight at the sight of her friend. Angelo was lying in a bed, his face pale. His dark hair clung to his forehead. He smiled weakly, but even wounded, the man was still undeniably gorgeous. She wasn't sure what she'd expected, but it was a lift to her spirits to see him sitting up a little and awake. Angelo grinned when he saw her, but the smile faded beneath his pain.

"*Bella.*" Hearing him speak her nickname made her eyes well with tears. Beautiful. He always called her beautiful. "My mother mentioned you were here," he chuckled, then winced.

"I wouldn't be anywhere else. Jared was here, but he was up all night with your family and completely exhausted. I sent him home to be with Felicity and Hayley. Thad is still in Orlando and can't get here until tomorrow. He texted me that he wants to video chat you as soon as you're up for it."

Angelo rolled his eyes. "Those two, they'll mother me worse than my *own* mother, and that's saying something."

"You're probably right." She laughed and then let out a huge sigh of relief. "I'm just so glad you're okay," she whispered and gave him a watery smile as she brushed away a few tears. She sat in the chair beside his bed and held his hand.

"Of course, I am," he teased. "What's a few knife wounds?"

"Don't joke about it; you could have died."

"But I didn't. I was given a second chance," Angelo said more seriously.

His gaze flicked to Roarke, who was hovering in the doorway.

"Roarke, I heard you were with Shana in Switzerland," he said, his brown eyes assessing Roarke with curiosity.

"We were, but when Jared called, we flew home immediately."

"I'm sorry I wrecked your trip and Christmas."

"There's nowhere I'd rather be," Roarke said, and by the look of surprise on Angelo's face, Shana knew he'd heard the honesty in his voice like she had. "And I hear you were quite the hero," Roarke added. "You did a good thing helping Kara, and this is what you got for it. Shit like that shouldn't happen to heroes. But it sounds like you will be okay."

"I should be," Angelo said. He was silent a moment before he looked at Shana. "Is Kara still in the lobby? My parents said that they thought she was."

"Yes, she's waiting to come see you after I'm done."

"Good." Angelo relaxed. "I need to make sure she's all right after what happened to her." It was just like Angelo to worry about someone else while he lay in a hospital bed.

Roarke cleared this throat.

"I'll just give you two some time to talk. Shana, I'll be in the waiting room if you need me." Roarke nodded at Angelo.

"Thank you, Roarke," Angelo said, and Shana knew her friend meant it.

"I was so scared when Jared called me," she told Angelo after they were alone.

When a tear slipped down her cheek, she brushed it away. She was exhausted, and in the last twenty-four hours she'd experienced every range of emotion a person could feel. Angelo had this way of making her open up in a way no one else did ... except Roarke.

"I heard you left a lovely Swiss ski resort for me. I wish you hadn't. You deserved a lovely holiday," he said with a gentle teasing that made her smile.

"Nonsense, I had to come."

Angelo turned her hand over so that he could curl his fingers around hers. "Put yourself first," he said. "It's time to let yourself be free. You don't need us to protect you from life."

She didn't understand. "But I do need you—"

"We'll always be here for you. Jared, Thad and I adore you. But we aren't what you need. You're starving, Shana. Starving for love."

Fresh tears burned her eyes, and she pulled her hand away from him, hurt beyond words by him.

"Starving for love? You make me sound pathetic."

Angelo shook his head.

"We all need love to survive and thrive. You deserve it like everyone else, and too many people have made demands of you that have kept you away from what you need."

The truth of his words pierced her so deeply that she couldn't speak.

"Someone out there needs you as much as you need him, and it's time to give him a chance."

"Who—"

Angelo's gaze flicked toward the door in the direction Roarke had gone, making it clear who he meant. "He's loved you for years; it's time you let his love in. We've been wrong about him—Thad, Jared and me. But it's not too late. He's still here, still in love with you. Don't let us get in your way."

He meant Roarke. She had known he wanted her, and he had shown how sweet and caring he was in the last two days. But that wasn't enough to throw her heart on the line, was it?

"You three gossip more than Felicity and I do," she told him. Imagining Jared, Thad and Angelo sitting around drinking beer and discussing her love life would have upset her before, but now she chuckled at the image.

"Men love to talk just as much as women do." Angelo winked at her. "Also it's Christmas; you shouldn't be here. I have all of my crazy family outside for me. You should be with the person you love. And who loves you back."

She tried to smile. "Are you telling me to go away on Christmas?" she asked. Angelo smiled.

"I am. Now, go away and be happy. *Be loved.*"

She stood and leaned over, kissing Angelo's forehead. "Rest up. I'll come and see how you are tomorrow."

His warm brown eyes twinkled with amusement. "Only if you aren't busy, and I hope *he* keeps you busy."

She rolled her eyes at his teasing and then with one gentle hug around his shoulders, she left the room. As she walked back to the waiting room, her steps slowed a little as she contemplated her next move. Her heart was pounding as she debated with herself what to do about Roarke.

Angelo was right. She needed to let go of the past and the safety net that the three protective men had provided her these last several years. She needed to reach for the future with someone who would make her truly happy. Being with Roarke for the last few days had given her more happiness than she'd had since she could remember. She couldn't let that go. Emboldened by her new sense of direction, she went to find Roarke.

The waiting room was empty except for Angelo's family, Kara and Roarke. They were all eating the food that Roarke had been so thoughtful to get for everyone. Roarke was speaking softly to Kara, and Shana was relieved to see the woman was finally eating and drinking something. She'd been sitting rigid all night in the same chair, clearly worried about Angelo because he'd ended up in the hospital trying to help her.

She made the rounds of goodbyes with Angelo's family and gave Kara a hug and told her to go see Angelo now that she was done. Then she stopped at last in front of Roarke.

"You okay, babe?" he asked as he immediately put his hands on her hips in a comforting but not possessive way. It filled her with a buzzy warmth that made her want to never let go of him.

"Yes, yes I am. Can you take me home?"

"Of course," he said as he pulled out his cell phone to call his driver while she grabbed her coat and his from the back of a nearby chair.

Roarke was quiet on the ride to her apartment, and so was she. She had a lot of planning to do if she wanted to get her life sorted out.

When the car stopped in front of her apartment, she leaned over and hugged him.

"Thank you for everything," she said.

"Do you want me to come up with you?" he asked. She knew the invitation wasn't sexual; he genuinely wanted to make sure she was okay.

"No, I have to do a few things on my own for a bit. Is that okay?"

"Of course. You know I'll be here if you need me." He looked away then, and she tried to ignore the stamp of guilt. She didn't want to push him away, but she needed to do some things on her own to prove she could.

"Merry Christmas," she whispered and kissed him on the check before she slipped out of the car and headed to her apartment building. It was time she took charge of her life.

7

Roarke entered his apartment, tossed his keys and wallet into a bowl on a table by the entryway and leaned back against the closed door. A soft sigh escaped him as he closed his eyes. He had tried to ignore the ache in his chest as he watched Shana walk away from him when he'd dropped her off at her place.

He knew she needed time and space to decide if she truly wanted him. He would never push her, even if she decided she didn't want him. But damn, he had gotten hopelessly addicted to her in the last two days. It was as he had feared—loving Shana up close was far more dangerous than loving her from afar.

He opened his eyes and stared around at his home, lost in thought. The loft was more of a penthouse than an apartment. He had bought the entire top floor of his friend's building when his friend had gotten married and wanted to move to the edge of the city.

Now, Roarke lived in a bachelor's dream home, with dark leather couches and stainless-steel appliances accented by black granite countertops. He had a California king bed with crisp white sheets. Roarke had always liked the minimalist, neutral tone style of his décor, but as he returned that Christmas night, the place felt cold and lonely. It would have been so different if he'd been able to take Shana home with him tonight.

After collapsing on his couch, he rested his head in his hands and drew in a deep breath, truly immersed in the hollowness of his solitude. He wanted Shana here, he wanted to cook her dinner, he wanted to make love to her and then curl up and watch TV with her in his arms. He wanted a thousand small, bright and beautiful moments that could never be bought with money, only love. He had *so much* love to give, and yet no one seemed to want him. Not the boys he had once craved as friends, nor the girl that had bewitched him all those years ago. No, he was alone on Christmas, *again*.

He stared at the wall, smothered in the silence for a long while before his cell phone buzzed. Work was always there when he needed a distraction from his loneliness. He poured himself a glass of scotch and took a drink before he decided to retrieve his laptop and work for a few hours.

He ended up doing this same thing every Christmas, not because he wanted to work but because with no family and no friends, he had little else to occupy him. There were only so many times he could watch Christmas movies on TV alone before he started to feel depressed. And this year it was far worse, because he'd had a taste of his dream life with Shana, and it had been taken away within a matter of days.

Burying himself in work for the next three hours, he barely noticed the passage of time until the antique clock on his fireplace chimed seven. He pushed the pile of legal folders full of real estate deals away and got up from the couch just as a knock sounded on the front door of his penthouse.

He went to answer it but saw no one through the peephole. Frowning, he opened the door a crack. A glint of red caught his eye, and he glanced down to see a fancy red box sitting in front of his door. The box moved slightly and whimpered. A flutter of sudden nervous excitement trickled through him. Presents left on doorsteps without a person bearing them were either usually really good...or really bad.

Hesitantly, Roarke reached down and unfolded the lid of the box... and his heart simply stopped. A chubby golden retriever puppy with a big red bow around its neck sat gazing up at him with soulful brown eyes. It whimpered a little and lifted a paw up at the side of the box, trying to get to him. It was exactly the type of dog he always wanted as a boy. Unable to resist, he bent and retrieved the puppy, lifting it up into his arms. It squirmed a moment before settling in to lick his chin vigorously. Roarke couldn't help but laugh. He couldn't remember the last time he felt this ... *happy* ... except when he'd been with Shana in Gstaad.

A sudden movement around the corner of the hall, near the elevator bay, caught his attention. Shana walked around the corner where she'd clearly been hiding. Her hands were tucked in the pockets of a long black coat as she walked slowly toward him. His heart leapt into his throat at the sight of her.

For the last few hours he'd been forcing himself to accept that she might never come back to him, that the few days they'd shared hadn't meant to her what they'd meant to him. Yet here she was ... at his door, with a puppy wearing the cutest damn bow, and he felt like couldn't breathe. Roarke was a second away from simply falling to his knees to beg her to never leave him, to confess that he loved her madly and would always love and cherish her the way no other man ever would.

"You like him?" she asked with a bashful smile that nearly killed him. Roarke ruffled the puppy's furry head.

"How can I not? He's just like Zeus, only a puppy…" He felt like the Grinch when his heart swelled ten times too large. It hurt to breathe, he was so happy.

"Good, because he's your Christmas present." Shana reached him and kissed the puppy's head and stroked one of his paws.

"Is he, now?" Roarke studied the puppy and then her, and saw how she was anxiously awaiting his reaction. "And what about you? Are you my present too?" he asked hopefully.

"You want me to be?" she asked coyly. But he could hear the quiet longing beneath her words.

He wanted to tell her that he desired her more than his next breath. But he was terrified she would change her mind and walk away.

"You know what they say," he began instead. "You give a man a dog, he's going to want a yard. If you give him a yard, he's going to want to home. And if you give a man a home … he's going to want a woman to love in it."

"Well, it's a good thing I want to be loved in a home with a man who has a yard and a dog." She smiled, and his heart pounded with excitement. She was here. She was saying she wanted to be with him.

"I didn't get you anything," he said quietly, feeling like a complete idiot. He could have managed to get her *something.* He'd been so focused on Angelo and getting her back to Chicago that he'd completely forgotten it was Christmas.

"You didn't get me anything?" she echoed. "Roarke..." The way she said his name, softly, sweetly, it nearly killed him. "You already gave me *everything*." She smiled, and his whole world was lit with the light from that single expression. "You really did love the lonely out of me. I finally feel wanted. I feel *cherished*. You gave me not only the most wonderful few days of my life in Switzerland, but you gave me back *hope*. You showed me that I am important, that I can and should take charge of my own life and that my happiness is under my control, not anyone else's. You didn't just give me romance; you gave me something infinitely more important. You showed me how to value myself. I'd forgotten somewhere along the way, and you gave that back to me. That's a gift that I can never repay." Her eyes glittered with happy tears.

Roarke held the puppy tight, wanting to put his arms around Shana too. He was speechless. Thankfully, she didn't seem to notice.

"I'm sorry it took me a little while to get here. I had to quit my job and then track down this little guy. Frankly, the fact that I managed it all on Christmas is a miracle itself." She brushed her fingers over the puppy's fur and he yawned, his pink tongue flopping out of the side of his mouth.

"Where did you find him?" Roarke couldn't imagine a single place being open on Christmas night.

"The retriever rescue society. Thank God, my friend Sarah works there, and she could get the place to open up long enough for me to fill out the adoption paperwork on a holiday. She loves a good story, and I told her about how you got me all the way here from Switzerland to see Angelo in time."

"This little guy is a rescue?" Roarke was touched by that. He knew that a lot of rescue societies existed for specific dog breeds. He'd read somewhere that a third of the dogs in shelters were actually purebred. It wasn't only mixed breeds that ended up in bad situations without homes.

"His mom was from a puppy mill. She thankfully had her pups at the society's shelter instead of the mill," Shana said. "They were able to give her and the puppies proper medical care."

"He'll have a good home ... with us." He added the last two words hoping she would agree. There was a part of him still convinced he'd fallen asleep while working on the couch and was dreaming all of this.

"Yes he will, *with us*," she agreed. "Are you going to let us in?" she asked Roarke. They were still standing in the hallway.

"Oh yeah, sorry. Come in." He opened his door, and she picked up the puppy's box and followed him inside.

"Did you really quit your job?" he asked as she set the box down and removed her coat.

"Yes, I went to my dad's office where I knew he'd be working, and I told him I was done. I want to work in family law, specifically in adoptions. I want to be passionate about my work. He didn't agree, and I said I didn't care if he agreed."

"That may be the hottest thing you've ever said." He grinned. He was proud of her. She had taken control of her life, and he wanted to be there to cheer her on for every decision she made from now until forever.

"Oh yeah?" She laughed softly.

"Yeah, when women go after what they want, it's *hot*."

Her gaze softened seductively. "In that case, I'm taking what I want now. *Tonight*."

"And what is that you want?" he asked, his voice deepening slightly

"You ... tonight, tomorrow, forever and a day after that." She gazed up at him with those eyes that always tore his world apart and put it back together. "I love you, Roarke. I love you so much it hurts, but it's the good kind of hurt, the kind that makes me know it's real. Only love can feel like this." She touched her chest with her hand.

Roarke swallowed thickly as a lump formed in his throat. "That's good, because I've felt that way about you ever since I first saw you. You're it for me. You're *everything* for me, Shana. I love you." He'd never said the word *love* that way before, and finally saying it to her, the woman who held his heart, it felt like he was back on the mountain peak looking down on the clouds below with sunlight and snow all around him. It felt like heaven.

She removed the sleepy puppy from him and set it down on a nest of thick blankets on the floor by the couch where it quickly fell asleep. Then she grabbed Roarke's sweater by the collar and pulled him toward her. Roarke's hands settled on her hips before sliding around to her ass and squeezing it hard. She moaned in pleasure.

"I think it's time I unwrapped my present," she whispered between long, hot kisses.

"I think that's a very good idea." He picked her up and she wound her legs around his waist as he carried her into his bedroom. As he lowered her onto his bed, she gazed up at him.

"Promise you'll always be a bad boy for me?" she asked.

As he leaned down and cupped her face in his hands, he winked at her. "I'll always be *whatever* you need. That's what *love* is."

"It is, isn't it?" She stroked his cheek. "I'll be that for you too. We're in this together from now on."

"Yes, we are," he promised. "I'm with you, *forever and a day*."

Outside, a light snow began to fall. The puppy in his bed of blankets slept deeply, dreaming of his bright, warm future where he would only know love. The three of them would be together. No more lonely holidays, no more empty beds and frozen hearts. Roarke, for the first time in his life, *loved* Christmas.

THANK YOU SO MUCH FOR READING *STRANDED WITH Prince Charming*! Stay tuned for Angelo's story *Finding Prince Charming*, the next book in the Ever After series!

ABOUT THE AUTHOR

Lauren Smith is an Oklahoma attorney by day, author by night who pens adventurous and edgy romance stories by the light of her smart phone flashlight app. She knew she was destined to be a romance writer when she attempted to re-write the entire *Titanic* movie just to save Jack from drowning. Connecting with readers by writing emotionally moving, realistic and sexy romances no matter what time period is her passion. She's won multiple awards in several romance subgenres including: New England Reader's Choice Awards, Greater Detroit BookSeller's Best

Awards, and a Semi-Finalist award for the Mary Wollstonecraft Shelley Award.

To connect with Lauren, visit her at:
www.laurensmithbooks.com
Lauren@laurensmithbooks.com

www.ingramcontent.com/pod-product-compliance
Lightning Source LLC
Chambersburg PA
CBHW030836200726
48285CB00007B/2458